LADY
DAISY

Dick King-Smith

Illustrated by Jan Naimo Jones

Delacorte Press

Published by
DELACORTE PRESS
Bantam Doubleday Dell Publishing Group, Inc.
1540 Broadway
New York, New York 10036

The text was originally published in Great Britain in 1992 by
Viking Children's Books, The Penguin Group.

LIBRARY OF CONGRESS CATALOGING IN PUBLICATION DATA

King-Smith, Dick.
Lady Daisy / by Dick King-Smith ; illustrated
by Jan Naimo Jones.
p.   cm.
Summary: Nine-year-old Ned faces a lot of teasing when he decides to
keep a Victorian doll that speaks only to him.
ISBN 0-385-30891-4
[1. Dolls—Fiction.   2. Sex role—Fiction.
3. England—Fiction.]   I. Jones, Jan Naimo, ill.   II. Title.
PZ7.K5893Lad   1993
[Fic]—dc20
92-21834
CIP
AC

Manufactured in the United States of America

April 1993

10 9 8 7 6 5 4 3 2 1

MVA

Contents

LADY
DAISY

1

In the Box Room

◆◆ **I**'m *bored!*" said Ned.

He stood with his hands in his pockets and his lower lip stuck out, staring out the window of his grandmother's sitting room.

Outside it was blowing half a gale, the heavens were emptying and the raindrops chased one another endlessly down the windowpane.

"When I was your age," said his grandmother, "we made our own amusements. Haven't you got a book to read?"

"Yes, but it's boring."

"Well, draw or do a jigsaw or a crossword puzzle or play a game of solitaire. Patience is something you could do with, Ned. You seem to expect to be entertained all the time. If you go on saying you're bored, I shall find you some work to do. Like cleaning the silver. Except that you'd make an awful mess of it."

Ned's grandmother put down her embroidery, took off her spectacles, and stood up.

"Talking of awful messes," she said, "has just given me a brilliant idea. It's something I've been meaning to do for ages, but I've avoided it. A filthy day like this would be just the time to tackle it, especially with a big, strong nine-year-old boy to help me."

Ned brightened at being called big and strong, but he was suspicious. Whatever it was sounded like hard work.

"I shouldn't bother, Gran," he said hastily. "I'll be all right. I'll find something to do."

"Too right you will, pet," said his grandmother. "We are going to clear out the box room."

"The box room?" said Ned. "Whatever's that? I didn't know you had one."

"Come on. I'll show you."

"But this is the attic," said Ned, when they had climbed three flights of stairs to the top of the old house. "Oh, Gran, we're never going to clear out all this stuff."

He looked around at the assortment of junk that stood on the boarded floor of the long narrow room directly below the roof. There were trunks and suitcases and hatboxes, bags of old golf clubs, some cases of stuffed birds, a number of framed paintings leaning against the wall, piles of old books, remnants of carpeting, and all manner of other things that Gran kept "because they might come in useful one day." Standing proudly above the rest was a dapple-gray rocking horse with flaring salmon-pink nostrils. A younger Ned had often ridden it when nosing about in the attic, and now he sat on its wooden saddle, his feet touching the ground, and urged it into squeaky action.

"I didn't know you called this the box room," he said.

"I don't," said his grandmother.

She picked her way toward the far end of the room, where there stood a tall, folding tapestry screen.

"Give me a hand to move this, can you, pet?" she said, and when they had done so, Ned could see that what had always seemed to be the end wall of the attic, was not. There was a little door in it, no more than four feet high, and when his grandmother had opened it and switched on a light within, Ned could see that there was yet another room beyond. It was filled from floor to ceiling with cardboard boxes.

There were hundreds of them, of all shapes and sizes, from boxes small enough to have held an alarm clock or a coffee mug to great cartons you could have put a week's supermarket shopping in.

"Gran!" cried Ned. "Whatever have you kept all these for?"

His grandmother grinned a bit sheepishly.

"You never know when you might need a box for something or other," she said. "But I have been in-

3

tending to clear the place out, honestly I have, Ned. For about forty years. I keep saying to myself, I must do it before they put me in my own one."

"Own what?"

"Box."

"I don't understand."

"Wooden box—coffin—you know."

"Oh, Gran!" said Ned.

"Comes to us all," said his grandmother. "But not for a while yet, let's hope. Come on, let's start." She bent to get through the low doorway. "No," she said, "on second thought, that's not a good idea. I may not be the tallest woman in the world, but ducking under there isn't going to do my back any good at all. Would you mind passing them out to me?"

"Course I will," said Ned.

He looked around the attic.

"Tell you what, Gran," he said. "If you open that window there, you can chuck them straight out as I give them to you, and they'll land on the lawn below. Save us carrying them all downstairs. Then we can have a bonfire."

"But they'll get wet outside."

"No, they won't. Look, the rain's nearly stopped, Gran."

So, for the best part of half an hour, Ned carried out box after box and passed them to his grandmother, and she threw them out the window with loud cries of

4

"Watch out below!" and "Timber!" and "Bombs away!" until at last the box room was almost empty.

"Nearly done, Gran," Ned said.

"How many more?"

"About a dozen."

"You can chuck those out while I'm going downstairs," said his grandmother. "And then shut the window and turn the lights off, will you?"

When the final box had gone spinning down, Ned took a last look through the box room's little door. Then he saw that there was still one left, a shoe box tucked right under the angle that the roof made with the edge of the floor. He pulled it out and saw that, unlike the rest, it was neatly tied up with string. It felt too heavy to be an empty shoe box. Ned undid the string and took off the lid.

Inside there lay a doll.

She was perhaps eighteen inches from head to toe, and dressed in an ankle-length gown nipped at the waist by a sash of pink silk. The gown was apple-green and patterned with circlets of flowers, little white flowers with yellow centers, and around one arm the doll wore a black velvet band. Her shoes were pink to match the sash, and on her arms were elbow-length white gloves.

Her hair was black and flowing, and her face was rosy-cheeked and rosebud-mouthed like all her kind, the closed eyes fringed with long dark lashes. As Ned stared at the doll, he heard his grandmother's voice

have overslept a little, I grant you, but I had expected to see Victoria, as usual."

"Who's Victoria?" asked Ned.

"My dollmother."

"Dollmother?"

"The little girl who looks after me. She is younger than you, I should say. How old are you, by the by?"

"Nine."

"Ah, Victoria is but five. Now, let me see, the last thing I remember her saying was that the dear Queen is dead. Is that not sad?"

"The Queen's not dead," said Ned. "If she was, Charles would be King."

"Charles?" said the doll. "History, I can see, is not your strong subject. Charles the Second died more than two hundred years ago. You'll be telling me next that the Queen's name is Elizabeth."

"Well, it is."

"Foolish boy! Why, my dollmother is named after our great Queen-Empress. For sixty-four years Queen Victoria has reigned over us, and now she is gone. Nothing will ever be the same again."

Nothing ever will be, thought Ned. Then he said, "What year do you think . . . I mean, what year is it —now?"

"Do you know nothing, Master Ned?" said the doll. "Why, it is 1901, of course."

"Oh," said Ned.

He forced himself to look into the wide blue eyes. It

was unnerving to be addressed without facial movement of any kind.

He summoned up his courage and said, very politely, "I'm awfully sorry, but I'm afraid I don't know what you are called."

"Strange," said the doll. "One would have expected Victoria to have told you."

She said nothing further but continued to stare expressionlessly until at last, in desperation, Ned said, "What *are* you called?"

"My name," said the doll, "is Lady Daisy Chain."

"Oh," said Ned.

Despite himself, he took hold of the doll's white-gloved right hand to shake it, and as he pulled, the arm, its upper part encircled by the black band of mourning for the late great Queen, moved stiffly forward on its shoulder-joint.

"How do you do?" he said.

2

Victoria and Sidney

At that moment, Ned heard his grandmother calling him.

"Coming!" he shouted, and to the doll he said, "Excuse me. I'll be back in a minute."

He returned the rigid arm to her side and, taking her gently by the shoulders, laid her back in the box. As her body moved toward the horizontal, so the long-lashed eyelids slid forward and blanked out the blue eyes.

"Is it all right to put the lid on?" he whispered, but she did not reply.

"Ned!" called his grandmother again, nearer now, and he ran hastily out of the attic, closing the door behind him.

"Sorry, Gran," he said when he reached her. "I was up in the attic."

"What for?"

"Just making sure I'd turned the lights off."

At first, when Ned turned off his own light that night, he could not get to sleep. His mind was in a whirl, and when he did drop off, his dreams were mostly unpleasant. In one, he himself lay in a huge cardboard box, and suddenly a short fat old lady dressed in black and wearing a crown on her head looked over the edge of it and said in a loud, plummy voice, "Who in the world are you?"

When he woke early next morning, he half felt that the whole business had been a dream. Quietly, so as not to disturb his grandmother, he climbed to the attic and opened the box room door. There was the doll, lying in her shoe box just as he had left her. He knelt beside it.

"Lady Daisy," he said, "wake up. It's me, Ned."

Silence.

"It *was* a dream," said Ned aloud. "I imagined it all. I must be going bonkers."

He suddenly felt enormously sad, and he picked up the doll and held her in front of him at arm's length. As she rose to the vertical, her eyes opened.

"Why," said Lady Daisy Chain, "it is Ned! Good morning. I trust you are well?"

"Oh yes, Lady Daisy, very well, thank you!" said Ned happily, as understanding burst upon him.

I've got it, he thought. *The moment her eyes close, she's fast asleep! And she stays like that till someone sets her upright. When I took her out of that box yesterday, she'd been asleep for . . . let's see . . . eighty-nine years! I wish I knew more about this five-year-old Victoria she talked about. Why did the girl suddenly lose interest in her and put her away in a box tied up with string?*

"Lady Daisy," he said.

"Yes, Ned?"

"This girl, Victoria—your dollmother—what was she like?"

"Was?" said Lady Daisy. "You mean, what *is* she like?"

"Oh, yes."

"She is a charming child, well-mannered and dutiful, and attentive to her lessons. She could teach you a thing or two, I daresay—about history, for example. As to her looks, she has fair hair worn in ringlets, and eyes much the color of my own. She is, however, not strong. Her constitution is delicate, and care needs to be taken of her health. Unlike her brother, Sidney, who is three years the elder. He is a sturdy scamp and always up to mischief. Tell me, Ned, have you any brothers and sisters?"

"No."

"Why then, you must seek out Sidney. He is almost

of your own age and always game for a prank. It will enliven your stay here."

"Oh, I'm quite happy being with you, Lady Daisy," said Ned without thinking, and he stood her carefully on a nearby table, pushing forward a pile of books to support her back. From this vantage point, the doll's direct gaze fell upon the rocking horse.

"Why," she said, "whatever is Victoria's beloved Dobbin doing up here in the attic? For that matter, what are we doing here? Pray take me downstairs, Ned, I beg of you."

Ned hesitated. Below, he heard the sound of movement and then the water tank at the other end of the attic began to gurgle, telling him that his grandmother was running her morning bath. Once she was safely shut in the bathroom, he could take Lady Daisy down to his own room, but even so, it would be better to be safe than sorry, for he had no intention yet of sharing his secret.

He picked up the doll off the table.

"We'll go to my room," he said. *But first,* he thought, *I'll prove this business of waking and sleeping once and for all.*

"Lady Daisy," he said. "Before we go, could you recite something for me? A poem perhaps?"

"If you would like it, certainly. There is a favorite of Victoria's that would serve."

"How many verses has it?" said Ned.

"Only two."

"Please say it," said Ned, and Lady Daisy began.

> "Here's Lettie in her coach and pair,
> With Puss, and Rose, and Jane the fair,
>   All going for a ride.
> For horses, brothers Tom and Jack,
> With cousin Fred to push at back,
>   While Carlo runs beside."

The moment she had finished the first verse, Ned tipped her backwards. Her eyes closed and she fell abruptly silent.

Quickly he placed her in the shoe box, put on the lid, and made his way down to his room. He closed the door, sat on the bed, opened the box and, taking out the doll, propped her upright and now open-eyed upon the bedside table. Immediately she continued:

> "I hope that Puss will sit quite still
> While they are going up the hill
>   That looks far o'er the plain.
> There they will rest and watch the sea,
> Its white waves dancing merrily,
>   And then come back again."

"Very nice indeed," said Ned. "You spoke it beautifully."

14

He heard the bathroom door open and the sound of his grandmother's footsteps coming along the corridor.

"It is kind of you to—" began Lady Daisy, and then fell instantly silent as Ned put her hastily into the shoe box and slipped it beneath the bed.

His grandmother stuck her head around the door.

"You awake?" she said. "Oh, yes, I can see you are. Bathroom's all yours."

After breakfast, they were having a walk around the garden. Gran was doing some pruning and Ned some deep thinking.

He looked up at the attic's dormer window, out of which the cardboard boxes had come sailing, and at the window of his own room directly below.

"Gran," he said, "how long have you lived in this old house?"

"Since I married your grandfather, nearly fifty years ago."

"He died when I was very small, didn't he?"

"Yes."

"I suppose I've always liked this house," Ned said, "but now I like it even more. I don't know why."

But I do, he thought.

"Just as well, pet," said his grandmother, "seeing it'll be yours one day."

"Mine?"

"Yes. Hasn't Dad explained to you about the entail?"

"The entail? What's that?"

"You don't know, eh? Well, I think it's time you did. After all, you're nearly in double digits. It means that this house, with its estate, can't be sold to anyone else. It's entailed, within the family. It belonged to your grandfather, and before that to his father and before that to his father's father, and so on."

"But now it belongs to you?"

"No, it belongs to your dad. He was the heir to the estate, but he and your mum are perfectly happy where they are, at your home, so they let me go on living here. But when I'm in my box—"

"Oh, Gran, don't!"

"All right, when I drop off my perch, if you like, then you will all come and live here. And in the same way, at some time—a long, long way in the future, we hope—this house will be yours."

For some time, while Gran plied her shears, Ned was silent. The whole idea was too big for him to grasp. That this house should one day belong to him. It seemed somehow linked to Lady Daisy.

At last he said, "Gran."

"Yes?"

"Your husband—my grandfather, I mean—I never knew his name. Was he called Sidney?"

His grandmother straightened up and turned to face him.

"No, no," she said, "my husband's name was Harold. It was *his* father who was called Sidney—your great-grandfather. Someone must have told you that and you got the generations muddled."

"So Sidney lived here?"

"Yes, of course."

"Oh. Did he have any brothers or sisters?"

"He had a sister, a younger sister. She would have been your great-great-aunt if she had lived, but she died of scarlet fever when she was very young."

"How young?"

"Oh, let me see, she can't have been more than five. Yes, that's right, she died in 1901, not long after the old Queen. She was called after her—Victoria."

3

Not 1901

Ned went up to his room while Gran was cooking lunch. He took the doll out of her box and lifted her up.

The moment her eyes opened, she continued the sentence she had been speaking nearly three hours before, just as though no time had elapsed.

". . . say so," she said. "You have nice manners. What boarding school do you attend?"

"I go to our local primary school," said Ned.

"How strange," said Lady Daisy. "Sidney is a boarder at one of the best-known preparatory schools in the country, and in due course he will go on to public school."

"Oh, our school's public," said Ned. "Anyone can go. And I'll be back there before long, it's nearly the end of the holidays. I'm going home tomorrow, my parents are coming to fetch me."

"Will they come by the railway?" asked Lady Daisy. "Or has your father one of these newfangled motor cars?"

I don't know about newfangled, thought Ned. *It's a Volvo station wagon with sixty thousand miles on it.*

"They'll come by car," he said, and then, though he had not planned to say any such thing at this moment, he suddenly added, "Will you come home with us?"

"On a visit, do you mean?"

"No, to stay. For always. To live with us. I should like it so much if you would."

"It is most kind of you to invite me, Ned," said Lady Daisy, "but such a thing is quite out of the question. My duty is to Victoria. Whatever would she do without me? She would have no one to push out in the doll's pram, no one to tuck up in the doll's bed, no one to read to, or recite to, or say her multiplication tables to. Whatever would the master of the house and the mistress and Master Sidney say, not to mention the governess and the nursemaid and the cook and all the other servants, to see Miss Victoria without her beloved Lady Daisy Chain? It is not only that my dollmother is devoted to me, you see, Ned. I am devoted to her."

"But . . ." said Ned, and stopped himself on the brink of saying *she's been dead for eighty-nine years.*

19

"I fear there are no 'but's," said Lady Daisy firmly. "My place is here."

In the afternoon Ned settled down in the sitting room with a book while Gran had a nap, but he wasn't reading.

What am I going to do? he thought. *I could put her back in the box room, inside the shoe box tied up with string, just as I found her, and no one would ever know. But that would be horrible—like murder. So I must tell Gran that I've found her. Then what? Well, ask Gran straight out if I can take her home with me, to keep. But she'll probably say, "A great boy like you, wanting a doll!" Or she'll decide she must stay here as a sort of family heirloom. Or perhaps she'll give her to some little girl, one of my cousins maybe, or she might even want to sell her, because I bet a doll that old is pretty valuable. Well, at least I can ask. But then what about Lady Daisy —supposing Gran does let me have her, I mean? She still believes that everything is just as it was in 1901. She has no idea that Victoria and Sidney and everyone else she was talking about have been dead and gone for donkey's years. I'll have to break it to her. It'll be a terrible shock. It might break her heart.*

And then, quite suddenly, he felt sure that—supposing she had one—it wouldn't, that Lady Daisy Chain was a brave and resolute person who would come to terms with the loss of her adored Victoria and accept instead the protection of another. *Me,* said Ned to himself. *I shall never forgive myself if I don't try. Now.*

Upstairs, he took the doll out of her box and carried her around the bedroom, trying to think how best to explain things to her.

"How very oddly this room is furnished," said Lady Daisy, as her gaze fell upon the simple divan bed with its duvet, the neat built-in closets and the general lack of furniture and fussy decoration in a modern bedroom.

"The bed—how low it is and how cold it looks. Why, the fireplace is boarded up, I declare, and as for the walls, where have all the pictures gone—the landscapes, the miniatures, the silhouettes? And the mantelpiece is bare of all its ornaments, and the gaslights— where are they? I do not recognize it at all."

By now they had arrived at the window, and Ned held the doll up to look out.

"Where has the cedar tree gone?" cried Lady Daisy.

"What cedar tree?"

"Why, there was a magnificent cedar of Lebanon just outside this window—the children had a tree house in it. And the row of elms beyond—not one to be seen. And where have the shorthorn cows gone? Whatever are those great black-and-white brutes grazing the home pasture, I never saw such creatures before."

"Those are holsteins," said Ned.

21

"And look," Lady Daisy went on, "there is some sort of monstrous contrivance in the wheatfield!"

"That's a combine harvester," said Ned.

"And what are those extraordinary structures that I see on the horizon?"

"Those are electrical towers. You see, Lady Daisy, it isn't actually 1901 anymore."

At that moment, with a sudden shattering roar of sound, a low-flying fighter aircraft flashed across the sky before them, at a couple of hundred feet and a modest 400 m.p.h.

Ned turned the doll around to face him and for a long moment she gazed at him in silence. Then she said, "Not 1901, I think you said. Ned, I am inclined to believe you. Pray, tell me then, what year is it?"

"It's 1990," said Ned. "When I first woke you, you said you must have overslept. In fact, you had been asleep a very, very long time."

"In that box?"

"Yes. In that box, tied up with string and left in a corner of the box room."

"But Victoria would never have done so cruel a deed."

Ned stood the doll upon the windowsill and, in a quite natural gesture, took both her small gloved hands, raising her arms toward him.

"Victoria died," he said gently. "Of the scarlet fever. In 1901. When she told you of the death of her name-sake, the old Queen, those were the last words she spoke to you. Her mother and father, I suppose, could not bear to be reminded of her by the sight of you, so you were put away."

Again there was a long pause while Lady Daisy stared at him, expressionless and unblinking as ever, out of those baby-blue eyes.

At last she said, in tones of wonderment, "1990! To think! Ninety years since the Relief of Mafeking."

Ned said nothing, since the remark meant nothing to him.

"That awful machine," said Lady Daisy, "that flashed across the sky just now, howling and screaming like a demon—what was that?"

"Just an airplane."

"An airplane?"

"Yes, a fighter, a Tornado actually, they're not all that fast."

"Really?"

"Oh, no. I mean, when a spacecraft is blasting off, it gets up to about 25,000 miles an hour—like the one they used when the first men landed on the moon in 1969, you know."

"I do not know," said Lady Daisy faintly. "Men on the moon? I am quite overcome."

"It must be an awful shock," said Ned. "You'd better lie down for a bit." And, without really thinking what he was doing, he laid the doll in her box.

"Lady Daisy," he said, "d'you mind if I show you to my grandmother?" But of course she did not reply.

24

After tea his grandmother said, "This time tomorrow, you'll be at home."

"I don't really want to go, Gran," Ned said.

"Afraid you'll have to—school starts soon, doesn't it? Anyway, I seem to remember you saying you were bored."

"That was before . . . oh, look, Gran, there's something I haven't told you."

"Oh?"

"Yes, when we were clearing out the box room, I found something. I'll go and get her."

"Her?"

"Yes, shan't be a minute."

"I found this," he said, when he came downstairs with the shoe box and, putting it on the table, removed the lid.

Ned's grandmother looked down at the sleeping Lady Daisy Chain, at her green gown with its pink sash and the black armband, at her pink shoes and her long white gloves, and gave a cry of surprise and delight.

"A doll!" she said. "What a beautiful doll and what good condition it's in, considering it must be Victorian, I should think, by the style of dress. And you found it in this shoe box?"

"Tied up with string. Wedged in a far corner."

"How strange. It must have belonged to someone in

the family, to some little girl of those times, perhaps to your great-great-aunt Victoria."

"Perhaps," said Ned.

"Isn't she lovely!" said Gran, and she reached into the box.

Oh, no, thought Ned, she's going to lift her up! And her eyes will open! And she'll speak! Oh, no!

"Oh, look," said Gran, "her eyes are opening. After all this time. You could almost imagine she was going to say something."

Oh, don't, Lady Daisy, please don't, thought Ned, and as though he had spoken out loud, the doll stared at his grandmother in utter silence.

"Where have you been hiding her?" asked Gran, putting the doll back into the box.

"In my room."

His grandmother looked at him consideringly.

"D'you like her?" she said.

"Yes. Very much."

"Have you given her a name?"

"Yes."

"What?"

"She's called . . . I call her Lady Daisy Chain."

"After the motif on her gown. How nice! And how clever of you to have found her, pet—I'm most grateful to you. I shall treasure her."

"Yes. I suppose she'd be worth a lot of money."

"Oh, loads, I should think, but that's not important. I should never sell her. She is obviously one of the family. She'd look awfully nice in that corner cupboard over there, don't you think? I've got some other bits of Victoriana in it already. You could see her up there, whenever you came to stay."

Despite himself, Ned felt the tears gathering. To think of Lady Daisy standing shut up forever in that glass-fronted cupboard, crying out perhaps to be released but unable to make herself heard!

He turned away so that his grandmother should not see his face, and looked out the window. Then he swallowed, and said quickly in a choked voice, "Please, can I have her?"

"For your own, d'you mean, Ned? To take home?"

"Yes."

His grandmother came up behind him and put her hands on his shoulders, and stared out over his head at the part of the lawn where once (though she did not know it) the great cedar of Lebanon had stood.

"Finders keepers, eh?" she said.

"It isn't that," said Ned, "and I don't mean for my very own, I mean—to look after. Like you said about this house, you know, that it has to stay within the family because of the what-d'you-call-it."

"The entail?"

"Yes. Lady Daisy Chain could be entailed. Only I'd take care of her for now. Could I, Gran?"

His grandmother turned him around and looked at him, and saw how near to tears he'd been, and smiled.

Then she picked up the shoe box with its green-gowned occupant and gave it to him.

She looked down at the doll.

"Off you go then, Lady Daisy," she said. "You'll come back here again one day."

"Oh, thanks, thanks, Gran!" said Ned.

Gran gently stroked the doll's long black hair.

"I wonder," she murmured, "what she would say if she could speak."

4

"A Capital Arrangement"

"That lady," said the doll to Ned when they were alone together again in his room. "Who is she?"

"That's my grandmother."

"Your grandmother!" said Lady Daisy in a shocked voice. "But she was wearing trousers!"

"She often does, usually, in fact. So does Mum. Nearly all women do nowadays."

"Extraordinary! You will be telling me next that men wear earrings and necklaces."

"Quite a lot do."

"Now come, Ned, do not tease. It is difficult enough for me to adjust, as it is. The sitting room, for example —how changed it appears. The walls once again almost bare of pictures, and as for the furniture—why, no

chaise longue, no chesterfield, no davenport, no canter-
bury to hold the sheets of music for the grand piano.
The piano is still there, yes, but its legs—they were
exposed! In my day they were always covered, each
with a little frill."

"Oh, come on, Lady Daisy," said Ned. "You're kid-
ding!"

"I can only hope," went on the doll, "that when
your grandmother does wear a dress, the skirts are of a
length to conceal her lower limbs. Only the ankles may
be revealed, as every lady knows. To show more to a
gentleman's gaze would be most improper."

"Things have changed," said Ned. "Fashions are different, you know."

"Everything is different, it seems to me. What, for
example, was that strange object in the corner of the
sitting room? A kind of large square box with a glass
window let into the front of it?"

"Oh, that's the television set."

"Television? What is that?"

"Well," said Ned, "first of all they invented radio—"

"Radio? What is that?"

"It's a machine that you switch on and then you can
hear people talking and music and all that. And then
they invented television, where you can hear people
and see them, too, in color. You can see things happening all over the world, live, they beam it by satellite. I
tell you what, Lady Daisy, I'll show you. I'll put the
telly on and you can see for yourself. We'll wait till

30

Gran's out of the way somewhere. Which reminds me. I'm ever so grateful you didn't speak to her when she picked you up."

"Why?"

"Because I want it to be our secret. I don't want you to talk to other people. I don't want them to know."

"Victoria was just the same. See, I said 'was' quite naturally. Poor little dollmother. To die so young. But she was always delicate."

"You mustn't be sad," said Ned. "It was all so long ago. I want you to be happy and I'll do my best to see that you are, if you'll let me. I asked Gran and she said I could take you home with me and look after you. Only, of course, I wouldn't unless you agreed to come. Will you?"

"You are a strange lad, Ned," said Lady Daisy, "to wish to have a doll. Why, Sidney and his playfellows would never have dreamed of such a thing. They were only interested in manly pursuits—making believe that they were soldiers of the Queen fighting the crafty Boers, or indulging in a bout of fisticuffs, or playing at cricket or soccer."

"Oh, I like soccer," Ned said. "I play for our school's First Eleven. I'm the goalkeeper."

"And now you wish to keep me?"

"If you would like that."

"To adopt me, in fact?"

"Yes."

They stared at one another. By now Ned had become used to the fact that looking into the doll's eyes told him nothing. That they were open showed she was awake, but as to what she was feeling, he had no clue. Since she could not move a muscle, there was no smile or frown on the smooth waxen face to guide him, but only the blank blue stare.

After a minute—ages, it seemed to Ned—Lady Daisy spoke.

"Very well, Ned," she said. "It seems to me that to become your adopted doll might be a capital arrangement, if that is what you really wish."

"I do, I do!" cried Ned delightedly.

He felt like hugging her, but she was much too small for such a demonstration of affection, and anyway, he thought, it would be sloppy, so instead he took her gloved fingers in his own, and said, "Shall we shake hands on it?"

"By all means," said Lady Daisy.

So they did.

"Now," said Ned, "you must be exhausted after all the excitement of today. Would you like to lie down?"

"Goodness gracious, no, dear boy!" said Lady Daisy. "I do not feel in the least tired. Eighty-nine years' sleep is enough to refresh anyone."

"What would you like to do then?"

"May we watch the machine of which you spoke? The 'telly,' I believe you called it."

"Yes, of course," said Ned.

He looked at his watch.

"Gran will be switching on the six o'clock news soon—she always sees that."

He carried Lady Daisy (upright, of course) out of his room.

"Sidney," she said as they came to the head of the stairs, "used always to slide down the banister. A daring lad, was Sidney."

Oh, rats to old Sidney! thought Ned, and he sat on the broad polished mahogany stair rail, a little nervously, to tell the truth, for he had never done this before, and pushed off.

Down they went, at such a speed that Ned came flying off at the bottom, almost cannoning into his grandmother, who was crossing the hall at that moment.

"Watch out, Ned!" she cried. "You nearly knocked me flying. And carrying that doll too. I thought you said you were going to take care of it. Supposing you'd dropped it? It's a wax doll, you know, its head is only made of hardened beeswax, it would have smashed into bits on the floor."

"Sorry, Gran."

"All's well that ends well. Switch on the telly for the news, will you, pet? I've just got to put something in the oven."

"Sorry, Lady Daisy," said Ned softly as they went into the sitting room.

"What for?"

"Well, you heard what Gran said."

"I did. But you would not have dropped me, Ned. Of that I feel certain."

Nonetheless, his grandmother's words had sent shivers down Ned's spine, and though he stared at the television, it was a blank stare. His mind was full of dreadful pictures, of Lady Daisy lying with a fractured skull, the blue eyes closed, never again to open, or, worse by far, of a headless corpse amidst smithereens of broken beeswax.

Unconsciously, he stroked the long black hair as she stood wedged between his side and the arm of the chair, gazing at the set.

"Oh, dear," said Gran as she switched off the set at the end of the news. "How I wish they could find something nice to tell us once in a while. It's all so depressing nowadays. Whatever would that doll think of the world today—if it could think?"

"Not *it*, Gran," said Ned. "She."

"Of course. Sorry, Ned. Sorry, Lady Daisy, will you forgive me?" But answer, of course, came there none.

"Well," said Ned later, back in his room, "what did you think of the television?"

"Perfectly amazing!" said Lady Daisy. "The strides that have been made in inventions! We had photographs, of course—how I wish I could show you one of my dear Victoria—but to see moving photographs, in color, of things actually happening as one watches! Unbelievable. And the things they showed. Those great airplanes that carry hundreds of people to places like America in a matter of hours, and those astronauts floating about and turning somersaults in the air, and those machines that know the answers to everything—what were they called?"

"Computers."

"Yes. So many new words to learn."

"Everything must seem so different," said Ned.

"Some things have not changed, it seems," said Lady Daisy dryly. "Except maybe to become worse. Wars everywhere, and cruelty, and famine. The human race may have learned a great deal, but apparently not much about loving their neighbors."

"Everyone must look very different."

"Yes, indeed—the clothes, or perhaps one should say the lack of clothes."

"Girls showing their legs, you mean?"

"Not only their legs. That picture of that winner of the beauty competition . . ."

"Oh, Miss World, you mean? In her swimsuit?"

"Is that what it is called? Unfortunately, I could neither look away nor close my eyes. Shameless!"

Downstairs, the phone rang.

"Ned," called his grandmother. "It's for you."

"Coming!" shouted Ned.

He propped the doll on a chair and ran out.

"It was the telephone," he said when he returned.

"It's a machine for talking to people who are a long way away."

"Oh, go and teach your grandmother to suck eggs!" said Lady Daisy rather sharply. "The telephone was invented a hundred and fifteen years ago, my dear Ned."

"Oh. D'you mean you had one, here in this house?"

"Of course. We were not savages, you know, even if we knew nothing of some of the benefits of today's civilization. To whom did you speak, if one might ask?"

"To my dad. They're coming to fetch me tomorrow morning."

"To fetch us," said Lady Daisy.

"Oh yes, yes!"

"And we shall travel in a motor car?"

"Yes."

"Along one of those motorways we saw on the news, where there was that dreadful accident?"

"Yes, but don't worry, Lady Daisy. Dad's a careful driver."

"But the speed they go! In my day a man carrying a red flag walked in front of the motor car. I confess I am nervous."

"Would you rather travel in your shoe box?"

"If you please, Ned. So much is happening to me, so fast. I am used to life at a far slower pace. And you must remember that now I am an elderly doll, very old in fact."

But you cannot die, thought Ned to himself—and then, remembering Gran's warning—or can you?

"You're not old, Lady Daisy," he said. "You're ageless. You're the most beautiful doll in the world!"

"Oh, Ned," said Lady Daisy, "how nice of you! That is what Victoria always used to say."

Do her cheeks look a little pinker than usual? thought Ned. No, it must be a trick of the light.

5

A Battered Old
Shoe Box

"I wonder what your father will say," said Gran next morning.

Ned had chosen a special breakfast—Gran always allowed him to do this on his last day—of two hard-boiled eggs squished up with a fork after adding a big lump of butter, and then muffins spread with more butter and Gran's homemade strawberry jam.

He swallowed his last mouthful and said, "Say about what?"

"About the doll."

"Oh, I don't suppose he had one, when he was my age."

"He most certainly did not. Your dad and his chums were macho types—always playing war games, or doing judo, or kicking a soccer ball."

"Sounds just like Sidney," said Ned, without thinking.

"Sidney? Do you mean your great-grandfather? How on earth do you know about him?"

"Oh, Sidney's a boy at school," Ned lied quickly.

He thought for a bit and then he said, "Dad doesn't have to know about Lady Daisy, does he?"

"You mean you'll take her in her shoe box?"

"Mmm."

"What about your mother? Is she to know? Or are you just going to keep the doll boxed up? Probably safer that way, then she can't be dropped or damaged."

"Oh, Gran, that won't be very comfy for her!"

"You're a funny boy," said his grandmother. "You really seem to have become quite fond of Lady Daisy Chain. Anyway, you can rely on me—I shan't say anything."

"Oh, thanks, Gran."

"Has he been good?" said Ned's mother at lunchtime.

"Good as gold," said Gran. "Though there's nothing much for him to do here; it's a bit boring for him."

"It's not, Gran," said Ned.

He caught her eye, and they grinned at each other.

"Well, it's back to school next week, Ned," said his father. "And this term you've got soccer to look forward to. Did you know, Mother," he said to Gran, "that Ned plays in goal for the school's First Eleven? He's their goalkeeper. Pretty good, eh?"

"A chip off the old block," said Gran.

Ned's father looked pleased, with himself as well as his son.

"I used to play on the wing," he said. "Pretty quick I was, though I say so myself. Now then, we must get a move on. I want to be through London before the worst of the rush hour."

"Have you packed your things, Ned?" said his mother.

"Yes, Mum."

Ned had only brought a small case, not roomy enough for his clothes and the shoe box as well. Anyway, he didn't like the idea of the box being inside anything, though common sense told him that if Lady Daisy had survived eighty-nine years without the need of a breath of fresh air, a couple of hours more wouldn't hurt. But he would tie the box up again with string, he thought, in case Mum or Dad should be nosy enough to take the lid off.

In his room, he lifted the doll up. Lady Daisy's eyelids slid silently back.

"Good morning, Ned," she said. "Or is it afternoon?"

"It's half past two," said Ned, "and we should be

home by five. Could you manage another little nap till then?"

"Let me have a last look out the window," said Lady Daisy, and then, "What is that great long white machine outside the front door?"

"That's our car," said Ned.

"Goodness gracious! To think that the last time I went for a drive, with Victoria, we were in the governess-cart behind the old gray pony. Put me to sleep, dear boy, I beg you."

Choosing the moment when his parents were saying farewell to his grandmother, Ned put his case and the shoe box quickly into the back of the Volvo and lowered the tailgate.

"Shut it properly, have you?" his father said.

"Yes, Dad."

"I'd better check."

Checking, he looked through the rear window and said, "What have you got in that box?"

"Something I gave him," said Gran quickly.

"Oh, a secret, eh? Come on then, say your good-byes."

"Thanks—for everything, Gran."

His grandmother hugged him as the others got into the car.

"Good-bye, Ned," she said, and as she kissed him, she whispered in his ear, "And good-bye, Lady Daisy. Don't forget, Ned, you're not just a goalkeeper, you're a dollkeeper."

Sitting behind his parents, Ned was thinking how difficult this business of secrecy was going to be, and for the first time in his life he felt the tiniest twinge of regret that he wasn't a girl. Then he would have had Lady Daisy on his lap for the whole journey, and could have held her up to the window to look out.

How astonished—and interested—she would be to see all the sights, so different, now in 1990, from everything she had known. *And I shan't be able to carry her around at home,* he thought, *like I could at Gran's— Dad would have a fit. We aren't going to get much chance to talk.*

Talking to Lady Daisy Chain, he realized as they sped along the motorway, had become a very important part of his life and something that he would miss dreadfully if it was to become impossible. He no longer thought of her as a doll, a toy, made in some long-demolished factory and clothed by some long-dead seamstress. She was a person, and an extraordinary person at that.

Last night they had talked for ages, or rather Ned had asked questions galore and Lady Daisy had answered them—all about life in 1901, what people had worn, what they had eaten and drunk, the games and sports they had played, the songs they had sung, their horses and carriages, their pets, their hobbies, their view of the world, a world so different from today's. A human would have had to be nearly a hundred years old to have known all those things, but in Lady Daisy's memory they were as fresh as paint.

How much he had learned from her already! *I bet I know more about those times than any of the teachers at school,* he thought.

"You're very quiet, Ned," said his mother from the front. "Are you all right?"

"Yes, fine, Mum. I was just thinking."

"A penny for your thoughts," said his father.

"I was thinking . . . about Gran," said Ned quickly. "How old was I when Grampa died?"

"You were . . . let's see . . ."

"Nearly two," said his mother.

"Yes, that's right, it must be nearly eight years ago that my father died."

"What was his name, Dad?"

"Harold."

"And what was *his* father's name?"

"My grandfather, you mean? He was called Sidney."

"Did he have any brothers or sisters?"

"He had one sister, but she died very young. Can't remember her name. You're very interested in family history all of a sudden."

"Gran was telling me about the entail. On the house."

"Was she now?"

"Yes, she said that when she dies, we'll go and live there."

"Would you like that?" said his mother.

"I wouldn't like Gran dying."

"That won't be for a long time, let's hope," said his father. "You'll probably be a grown man by then, maybe with children of your own."

I've already got a child, thought Ned, *an adopted one. Except that no one could call Lady Daisy a child. She may look like one, with her plump pink cheeks and her baby-blue eyes, but really she's a woman, a wise little old woman.*

That evening, in the safety of his own bedroom in his own home, he untied the string, took off the lid and lifted the wise little old woman out of her box.

Neither his father nor his mother had referred to it again as he was taking it out of the car, and with a bit of luck, he thought, they'll forget all about Gran's "secret" present.

"Welcome, Lady Daisy," he said, as the doll opened her eyes. "I hope you'll be very happy here."

"How kind of you, Ned," she replied. "Now, this is your own room, I presume."

"Yes. Mum and Dad call it my 'bed-sitter.' Let me show you around."

"What a fortunate young man you are, to be sure," said Lady Daisy, when the tour of inspection was over.

Ned had carried her slowly around the long low bedroom and pointed her in every direction, to show her, in addition to the bed, his little desk where he did his homework, his quarter-size pool table, his hi-fi system and, faced by a comfy old armchair, his own small portable TV set.

"Why, you even have your own telly!" the doll went on, and she sounded rather pleased.

"I know," said Ned. "Mind you, I'm only allowed to watch at certain times."

"But you will allow me to watch also?"

"Of course!"

"How different this room is," said Lady Daisy, "from the one in which you slept at your grandmother's. For one thing, you have so many pictures."

The walls of Ned's bedroom were papered with large blown-up posters of rock stars and soccer players. The largest of all was a huge photograph of a track-suited figure with dark curly hair, at full stretch in mid-air, his gloved fingers edging a soccer ball around the outside of a goalpost.

"Who," said Lady Daisy, "is that handsome gentleman immediately above your bed? Is he one of those astronauts? He appears to be flying."

"That's the England goalie," said Ned. "That's what I dream of being, one day. And talking of dreams, Lady Daisy, I remember you saying that you used to have a doll's bed. When you were with Victoria."

"Indeed. With silken sheets, and blankets of pure wool, and the warmest of eiderdowns. Not that I remember lying in it, of course, for I was always asleep the moment my head touched the pillows."

"I suppose they still make such things," said Ned. "Would you like a new one?"

"Why, no, Ned, thank you. It would be a waste of your pocket money. When I am not awake and talking with you, then I do not care two pins where I lie. And I think I have grown quite fond of that rather battered old shoe box."

At that moment, Ned heard footsteps on the stairs.

"Sorry, Lady Daisy," he whispered hastily. "I'll have to put you in it now."

Quickly he did so, and slipped the box under his bed.

"Ned," said his mother, coming into the room, "could you be very kind and let me have something I need?"

"Of course, Mum. What?"

"Well, you know that present that Gran gave you?"

"You can't have that," said Ned hurriedly.

"I don't want it, Ned—I've no idea what it is and I don't want to know unless you wish to tell me. It's simply that I'm packing up a present for Aunt Lucy— it's her birthday next week—and the thing that I'm giving her is just the right size."

"Right size for what?"

"Why, to fit in that box. That's all I'm asking you for, Ned—one rather battered old shoe box."

Secrets Everywhere

"But . . . but Gran gave it to me," said Ned. "I mean, she didn't just give me . . . what's inside it, she gave me the box too. It's part of the present. I promised to look after it, you see."

His mother sat down on the edge of his bed and looked at him thoughtfully.

"I don't see, Ned," she said. "But if the old box is so precious, why, you keep it of course. I'll find something else. Where is it anyway?"

"It's under the bed."

Ned's mother stood up again and smiled at him and gave him a hug, saying, "Funny old boy! Now then, I think you should be *in* the bed. It's been a long day and it's getting late."

Ned was suddenly filled with a mixture of feelings

—pleasure at being hugged, relief at not having to give up the shoe box, a sort of guilt at being so secretive about its contents, and a kind of pride in the possession of Lady Daisy and a wish to show her off.

He knelt down and slid out the box, and put it on the bed and opened it.

"That's what Gran gave me," he said.

"Oh, what a beautiful doll!" his mother cried, just as his grandmother had, and then she listened as Ned told her of the clearing out of the box room, and how he had at first kept his find a secret from Gran, and then showed it to her. "And Gran said I could look after her, you see, Mum."

"I had a doll when I was a little girl," said his mother. "Not as old as this one or as splendidly dressed, but I was fond of her. When you picked her up, she opened her eyes and said 'Mama' in a squeaky voice. What's this one called?"

"Lady Daisy Chain."

"What a lovely name. May I pick her up?"

"If you like."

As she was lifted up, Lady Daisy's eyes opened wide, but no sound came from her.

"Lovely blue eyes," said Ned's mother, "but she doesn't say anything."

"It'd give you a shock if she did," said Ned. "Just imagine—a doll that could talk to you!"

His mother laughed, and laid Lady Daisy back in the box.

"It's a pity you can't, my girl," she said. "You could tell Ned to get you something better to lie in than this old thing."

She put on the lid.

"Oh, she's quite happy with it," said Ned.

"She told you so, I suppose! Anyway, come on, it's time you were in bed. Better hide Lady Daisy before Dad comes up to say good night. He'd have a fit."

"He doesn't have to know, does he?" said Ned.

"Who doesn't have to know what?" said a voice just outside the door, and as Ned's father came into the room, his mother, with one quick movement, slipped the box beneath the bed.

"Just a little confidential matter," she said, as she made a show of arranging the bedclothes.

"Secrets everywhere today," said Ned's father in a mock-grumpy voice. "I suppose I shall be the last to know. Come on then, Ned, early bed for you."

"Can't I watch some telly?" said Ned.

"Not tonight," said his father. "Tomorrow you can stay up and watch *A Question of Sport* downstairs."

"Upstairs," said his mother firmly.

Later, when he knew his parents were safely settled below, looking at whatever program they had managed to agree upon, Ned took Lady Daisy out.

The previous Christmas a well-meaning aunt, knowing that he liked reading, had given him a pair of

large wooden bookends, carved in the shape of elephants. Ned had not quite known what to do with
them, since his books were all happily arranged on
shelves, but now he suddenly realized how useful they
would be.

He set them on his bedside table, and between
them he stood Lady Daisy, firmly supported now on
either side by an elephantine bottom.

"So," she said. "That was your mother?"

"Yes. Wearing trousers, I'm afraid, Lady Daisy."

"I am becoming used to that. How short she wears
her hair. Victoria's mother's was so long that she could
sit upon it. She brushed it a hundred times every night.
I have not seen your father, by the by."

"No."

"Though he may have seen me? Asleep, that is?"

"No."

"Would I be correct, Ned, in thinking that your father would consider that dolls are strictly for little
girls?"

"Yes, Lady Daisy. You would be right."

"What shall you do about that?"

"I don't know."

Downstairs, Ned's mother and father were watching a
situation comedy, in which the situation was boring and
the comedy just wasn't funny.

"That present that Mother gave Ned," said his father. "I wonder what it was."

"I wonder."

They watched a little longer, their faces expressionless, while the studio audience yelled with laughter.

"I've got it," said Ned's father suddenly.

"Got what?"

"What was in that box. I bet I know. I bet you all Lombard Street to a china orange, as Bulldog Drummond used to say."

"What was it then?"

"It's simple. It was a shoe box. And what comes in shoe boxes? Answer—shoes. Or more probably cleats. I bet she's bought him a new pair of soccer cleats."

"How clever you are," said his wife.

Upstairs, Ned was saying, "D'you think I ought to tell Dad, Lady Daisy? Own up, I mean?"

"You make it sound as if looking after me was a grave sin, to which you must confess," said Lady Daisy rather tartly.

"Oh, no . . . It's just that Dad would expect me to have the kind of . . ." he paused, not wanting to use the word "toy."

"Toy," said Lady Daisy.

"Well, yes, that most boys would have. Some kind of action man like Rambo, or a funny animal like Garfield or Kermit. If he knew about you, he'd think I was a wimp."

"Rambo? Garfield? Kermit? Wimp?" said the doll. "Have some mercy, Ned. These names are all double Dutch to me. But I do see your problem. Your father sounds to me very much a man's man. No doubt Sidney grew up in that mold."

"So what should I do?"

"My advice is twofold, Ned," said Lady Daisy. "First, I think that you should tell him. Secrets in a family are not good. Second, do not tell him yet. Wait for a favorable moment, one at which he might be especially proud of you, for example after an outstanding performance at some sport. In his admiration, he might be persuaded to overlook the fact that you have a doll in your room. That is all he need know, dear boy—that your grandmother, in a generous but possibly misguided gesture, gave you a doll, which you did not like to refuse and which you therefore felt you must keep in your room. Surely he cannot object to that?"

"How clever you are," said Ned.

"And as for your playmates," said Lady Daisy, "should you fear being thought a namby-pamby, why, it is not as though you were going to take me to school with you."

But, some weeks later, that is just what Ned did.

7

The Project

The very first day of the term Ned's teacher, Miss Judge, had announced that the class project was going to be "Life in Victorian Times."

"It was all very different in those days," she said. "There are so many things we take for granted now that the Victorians didn't have. No motor cars, for example, or only a few very early primitive ones, no airplanes, no television, no radio—"

Ned's hand shot up.

"Yes, Ned?" said Miss Judge.

"But, please, miss, at least they had phones. The telephone was invented a hundred and fifteen years ago."

After this had been checked in the encyclopedia, the teacher agreed that he was absolutely right. But she looked very surprised, and rather suspicious, so Ned decided he had better play things more carefully. Nevertheless, as the project progressed, Ned's pieces of writing and Ned's pictures and even Ned's poetry (for he could not resist including "Here's Lettie in Her Coach and Pair") were far and away the best in the class.

"This is really very promising, Ned," Miss Judge said when the project was a month old. "You certainly have a feel for those times. I don't know how you get all the details correct."

She would have known all right, if she could have been a fly on the wall in Ned's bedroom of an evening, and heard Lady Daisy, propped on Ned's desk between her elephant supporters, giving him the benefit of her knowledge.

One day Miss Judge handed out copies of a note for each child to take home.

"What's it about, Mum?" asked Ned.

His mother read it out:

"Dear Parent,
Class Two is doing a project on Life in Victorian Times and we plan to have a display of materials of that era. Any help that parents can give will be greatly appreciated. Books, toys, old photographs, clothes, and household objects will be welcomed and

great care taken of them. We should need the loan of them for the whole of the week before half-term.

"Well, that's an easy one for you, Ned. You can take Lady Daisy."

"Oh, no, Mum!"

"Why ever not? If it's Victoriana that your teacher is looking for, then Lady Daisy will be the star of the show!"

"But she'd be in there for a whole week!"

"So what?"

"She might get . . . damaged."

"Nonsense, everything will be taken good care of, Miss Judge says so. You'd be rather selfish if you didn't take her—think how interested the other children would be, especially the girls."

"It's not the girls I'm worried about," muttered Ned.

"Ah, I see, it's all your soccer friends you're thinking about, poking fun at you for bringing a doll. Look, you don't have to say it's yours. Simply say that it belonged to your grandmother, which is true, in fact."

"Not *it*, Mum," said Ned. "*She.*"

"Okay. *She.* Well, it's up to you, but I really think you ought to take her in to school."

I don't want to, thought Ned. *I don't want to one bit. Some of the boys will really beat up on me. Especially Troy Bullock.*

Troy Bullock was the captain of the school's soccer

team, who took pride in being a "hard man" on the field and modeled himself on Vinny Jones. Ned was tall for his age (useful for a would-be England goalkeeper), nearly as tall as Troy, but he was slight by comparison. He could just hear Troy sniggering, "Ned's got a dolly!"

A possible way out occurred to him. Lady Daisy might object to the idea of going to school.

"I should be most interested," said Lady Daisy that evening when Ned had reluctantly asked her how she felt about the whole business. "I should *very* much like to go."

"But how will you get any sleep? Miss Judge won't let me put you in the box, I don't expect."

"Sleep is not necessary to me, Ned, as it is to you. I am not capable of becoming fatigued."

"But I shan't see you for a whole week!"

"Yes, you will. You will not see me in the evening as you now do, but you will see me in the day as now you do not. It is six of one and half a dozen of the other."

"But I shan't be able to talk to you."

"True, but the time will soon pass. Time does, I can assure you."

"*You* won't speak, will you?"

"Of course not."

"But then what about my project?"

"Your folder for the project is almost finished, I think. You must manage on your own for a while, as you did before I came. Why, I am quite excited, I declare! I used to attend Victoria in the schoolroom when she had lessons from her governess, but I have never been inside a proper school. Life is very hard there, I remember Sidney saying, with long hours of learning, and meager food, and iron discipline. Sidney used to be beaten with a cane for the slightest misdemeanor. You must see to it, Ned, that I am placed upright in a commanding position so that I may observe all that is going on."

Ned fired a last shot.

"It will be awful without you," he said pitifully.

"Absence makes the heart grow fonder," said Lady Daisy.

The children of Class Two were told to bring in their bits of Victoriana on the following Monday. Ned took Lady Daisy Chain to school carefully wrapped in tissue paper, inside a Marks & Spencer shopping bag.

"Will that be all right?" he had said to her. "You won't need your shoe box because you'll be standing up all the time."

"But you wish me to be concealed during the journey to school?" said Lady Daisy.

"If you don't mind," said Ned.

He could just imagine meeting Troy Bullock and some of his cronies while he was carrying the doll in his arms.

"I am perfectly agreeable, dear boy," said Lady Daisy.

Was there a shade of amusement in her voice, Ned wondered.

One by one any child who had brought something took it to Miss Judge to show her. She was delighted to find that there was a really good selection of objects.

Most of them, like an old biscuit tin with a picture of Queen Victoria and Prince Albert on its lid, were genuine pieces of the period. One or two, however, were not; for example a 1953 coronation mug, brought in by a girl who had got her queens confused.

One of the first objects to be handed in was an antimacassar.

"Gentlemen of those days," said Miss Judge, "used to smear their hair with Macassar oil. So to keep the material of a chair from becoming stained and greasy, this would be draped over the back."

And then there was a host of other things—an oil lamp, a flatiron, a rolling pin, a stone hot-water bottle, a clay pipe, a candlestick with a snuffer, a little network lady's bag called a reticule, some books, some toys, and some old brown photographs.

"Wonderful!" said Miss Judge when all these had been arranged. "Now, is that the lot?"

All this time Ned had sat with the Marks & Spencer shopping bag between his feet, Lady Daisy lying asleep within. *I needn't bring her out,* he kept saying to himself. *I can leave her in the bag and just take her home*

*again after school and put her in her box. Mum will
think she's at school.* But then he recalled Lady Daisy's
words. *"I should* very *much like to go,"* she had said.

He put his hand up.

"I've got something," he said.

If only he had handed Lady Daisy in early, or
among the press of other children anxious to show the
teacher their treasures, he would not have attracted so
much attention. As it was, the eyes of the entire class
were upon him as Miss Judge called out, "Bring it here
then, Ned," and he marched up to her desk and handed
her the shopping bag.

Reaching in and removing the tissue paper carefully, she took out Lady Daisy.

"Oh, what a beautiful doll!" Ned's teacher cried,
just as his grandmother and his mother had. "And look,
her eyes open! Look, children! Why, that's lovely, Ned,
she'll be the star of the show. I didn't know you had a
little sister."

"I haven't," said Ned.

Somebody giggled.

"It's your doll then, is it, Ned?"

Everybody giggled.

Ned hesitated. The teacher was holding Lady Daisy
in such a way that the blue eyes were staring straight
into his, and he knew, he just knew, that he should not
deny his ownership. But his courage failed him.

"Oh, no," he said, "it's not mine. It belonged to my
grandmother."

"It must be very valuable," said the teacher. "And that applies to a lot of these things, children, so get it into your heads here and now that all these objects may be looked at, but *not* touched. The last thing we want is for something to be broken or damaged in any way. Understood?"

"Yes, Miss Judge," everybody said.

So now Class Two's project on Life in Victorian Times was almost complete. The walls of the classroom were lined with the children's written work and paintings, and the exhibits were all arranged on a long table, with Lady Daisy Chain standing proudly in the very center. Nearly all the girls looked longingly at her, while the boys were most interested in other, different, toys—a popgun, a model of Stephenson's locomotive "The Rocket," a group of lead soldiers. They did not think to tease Ned about the doll—it wasn't his, after all, but his grandmother's. Ned thanked his stars that Troy Bullock was in Class One.

Each day that week he came early to school, hoping to have a word with Lady Daisy before anyone else arrived, but someone always did.

He waited impatiently for Friday, for school to finish, so that he could take the doll home.

All might have been well had not Miss Judge, on Friday morning, decided to ask Class One's teacher to bring her children in to see the exhibition. Each item

was labeled with its description and the name of the child who had provided it, so at Lady Daisy's feet there stood a small square of card reading:

VICTORIAN WAX DOLL

NED

Troy Bullock stood in front of this, pointing and nudging his pals, Ned saw, and he cringed.

All might still have been well had it not been raining hard all through lunchtime, so it was too wet to go out in the playground.

Choosing a moment when the teacher on duty was not around, Troy Bullock slipped into Class Two's room.

"Fancy Ned having a dolly!" he said loudly, and he picked Lady Daisy off the table.

"You're not allowed to touch!" cried some of the girls, but Troy took no notice. Instead he began to tip the doll slowly back and forth, making her eyes open and shut.

Ned went hot and cold at the same time, with anger and also with fear, for he knew he was no match for the great Troy Bullock in a fight.

"Here, stop that, Troy," he said in a croaky voice. "You might hurt her."

In answer Troy began to shake the doll faster and faster so that the eyelids were in constant motion.

"You want your dolly, Ned," he said, "you come and get it."

"It's not *his*," said one of Ned's friends. "It belonged to his grandmother, didn't it, Ned?"

The sight of poor Lady Daisy being manhandled, her eyes opening and shutting at high speed, was more than Ned could bear, and the cold fear went, leaving only the hot anger.

"Yes, it did once," he said. "But now it's mine. It's *my* doll."

Troy stopped shaking Lady Daisy and put her down on the table.

"What did I tell you?" he said, grinning. "It's Ned's doll. And only girls have dolls. So Ned's a big girl."

Afterward Ned could never think exactly how it happened. He couldn't really recall his arm shooting out and his fist landing smack on Troy's nose, while all the children gaped and gasped, and the teacher on duty came rushing in. But he always remembered very clearly, and with much pleasure, the sight of Lady Daisy's tormentor sitting on the floor, the blood running down his shirt, and then the look on everyone's face as the "hard man" of the school's First Eleven burst into floods of tears.

"That'll Teach Him!"

"Ned's been in a fight," his mother said when his father arrived home from work.

"In a fight?"

"Yes, at school today. His teacher rang up. She said the principal would like to see you about it, after half-term. The parents of the other boy concerned were pretty angry apparently."

"What was this fight about? Do you know?"

"Yes, I know. But I think you'd better let Ned explain."

"I think you'd better let me explain," Ned had said to Lady Daisy when they arrived home from school.

When he had returned from the headteacher's study, the other children in Class Two had all packed up their exhibits, and Lady Daisy alone remained, lying peacefully asleep on the table. Only now was he able to tell her what had happened.

"An explanation," she replied, "would be welcome, Ned. Being shaken into and out of sleep by that large, unpleasant boy was the most disagreeable experience of my life. I thought I should lose my reason. Why did you not intervene?"

"I did, Lady Daisy. I hit him."

"You struck the rascal?"

"Yes."

"With a straight left? Sidney used to say that a straight left to the jaw was the answer to such fellows."

"Well, actually, I hit him with my right hand. On the nose."

"Did it bleed?"

"Yes."

"Capital, capital!" cried Lady Daisy. "'Pon my word, I am proud of you, dear boy! We should mark the occasion in some way, but how? I know! You shall relieve me of this black band that I have worn upon my arm for so long."

Ned found a pair of nail-scissors and carefully snipped through the little ring of velvet.

"That is better," said Lady Daisy. "I have mourned

long enough for the old Queen. Let me rejoice for my gallant young prince."

Ned was sitting and Lady Daisy standing in the comfy old armchair, watching *Neighbours,* when Ned's father came in.

"I want to talk to you, Ned," he said. "Turn that rubbish off."

Ordinarily, Ned would have defended the program, which was a favorite of his. (As it was indeed of Lady Daisy's. "Life in Australia seems to be very interesting," she had said when first she saw it.)

But now he could see that his father was not best pleased, so he did as he was told. He did not attempt to conceal Lady Daisy, knowing that everything must now come out.

His father stared at her in horror.

"What in heaven's name is that?" he said.

"It's a doll, Dad."

"I'm not blind," said his father. "I should just like to know what you are doing with a doll."

"Gran gave her to me."

"My mother . . . gave you . . . a doll?"

"Yes."

"Was that what was in that shoe box you brought home?"

"Yes."

"Whatever made her do such a thing?"

66

"I asked her, Dad. I asked her if I could have Lady Daisy. That's her name, Lady Daisy Chain."

His father shook his head in disbelief. The look on his face was one of shock and disapproval.

"Let's leave that for the moment," he said. "Now then, what's all this about you getting into a fight? First of all, who was it with?"

"A boy."

"I hardly expected you to be punching girls."

He looked toward Lady Daisy, who was regarding him straightly from the chair.

"Though it's more likely you spend your time with them, by the look of things. Who was it you were fighting then—some poor little chap half your size?"

"No, Dad," said Ned. "The biggest boy in the school."

"Was it?" said his father in an altered tone. "Was it indeed? Was he bullying you?"

"Sort of. But really he was bullying Lady Daisy."

"Whatever do you mean?"

So Ned told his father the whole story, about the project, and taking the doll to school, and how Troy Bullock had been mistreating Lady Daisy.

"And he said I must be a big girl, to have a doll," Ned finished. "Which is what you're thinking, Dad, really, isn't it?"

His father hesitated.

"Well, no, not if you had a go at him, he sounds as if he deserved it. A lot bigger than you, is he?"

"Quite a bit."

"Well, that was gutsy of you, but you should try not to go around hitting people. You don't seem to have suffered much damage."

"I haven't. I just hit him on the nose and that was that."

"Did it bleed?"

"Yes."

"Well, I guess that'll teach him—he won't tangle with you again in a hurry. I like to think you take after me, Ned—able to stand up for yourself. I even did a bit of boxing when I was your age."

"But I don't suppose you had any dolls."

"Ah, well, I'm beginning to look at that in a different light now that you've told me the whole story. I see now that this doll is . . . well, kind of out of the ordinary . . ."

"Yes, she is."

"Because Gran gave it . . . her . . . to you."

"Well, she's sort of entailed—like Gran's house—and it's my job to look after her, Gran said, and that's what I was doing. But the principal wasn't a bit pleased, Dad, and nor were Troy's parents, Miss Judge told Mum."

"Oh, don't worry about that, Ned," his father said. "You did the right thing. I'll sort all that out for you. Which hand did you hit him with, by the way?"

"My right one."

"Haven't damaged it, have you? A goalkeeper needs to take care of his hands."

"No, it's just a bit sore."

"Not as sore as the other kid's nose, I bet," said his father.

He picked Lady Daisy out of the armchair and held her up in front of him.

"Pretty little thing," he said in a jolly, slightly embarrassed voice, and he went out of the room.

"A fine figure of a man!" said Lady Daisy as the door closed. "Let us hope that you will grow up to be as tall and broad-shouldered. I must say, it is a relief that he now also knows of my presence in the house. I realize you had no option, Ned, but it has been a trifle wearing suddenly to be thrust into that box on so many occasions, often in the middle of a conversation. Now everything is out in the open."

"Well, not everything, Lady Daisy," said Ned. "They don't know you can talk. You won't speak in front of them, will you?"

"You are continually asking me that, dear boy. What you have never understood is that it would make not the slightest difference if I did. Victoria and I would converse freely in front of her parents, or Sidney, or the governess, or any of the servants, and they were none of them any the wiser. They simply heard a little girl talking to her doll."

"I don't understand how that can be so."

"My dear Ned," said Lady Daisy, "there are more

things in heaven and earth (as Hamlet said to Horatio) than are dreamt of in your philosophy. May I suggest that, since your father now appears to have accepted your guardianship of me, you should make bold to take me downstairs, to a meal perhaps, in the bosom of the family. Then you will see what I mean."

So next morning Ned took Lady Daisy down to breakfast. He sat her on the table, propped against a box of cornflakes, and she joined in the conversation with a will. Yet neither his mother nor his father appeared to hear a word.

"Oh, you've brought the doll," his mother said. "Good morning, Lady Daisy. I hope you are recovered from your dreadful experience?"

"Quite recovered, I thank you," replied the doll, and Ned, listening, held his breath, but his mother went calmly on pouring out coffee and his father did not look up from his newspaper.

"Mrs. Thatcher's going to Moscow, I see," he said from behind it.

Ned said nothing.

His mother said, "Oh, really?"

Lady Daisy said, "I cannot get used to the idea of a woman as Prime Minister. A woman's place is in the home, would you not say, Ned?"

"Yes, I suppose it is," said Ned without thinking.

His father looked over the paper.

"You suppose what is what?" he said.

"Oh!" said Ned. "Um . . . I suppose . . . it is Saturday."

"Whatever's the matter with you?" said his mother. "Eat your breakfast, do."

"Children should be seen and not heard," said Lady Daisy. "That is what Sidney and Victoria were taught— sit up straight, chew each mouthful thirty times, and no talking at the table."

"How she does boss everyone about!" said Ned's father.

He must have heard her, thought Ned in a panic, he must have heard Lady Daisy!

"Why, did you hear what she said, Dad?" he said.

His father put down the newspaper.

"What *are* you talking about, Ned?" he said. "How could I *hear* what Mrs. Thatcher said? I read it—in this paper. Honestly, that doll's got more brains than you."

9

Goalkeeping Practice

N ed's grandmother rang up next day.
"Gran wants to speak to you," his mother
called.
Ned came to the phone.
"Hello, Gran."
"Hello, pet. How are you?"
"Fine, thanks."
"And Lady Daisy Chain?"
"Yes, she's fine too."
"Does Mum know about her yet?"
"Oh yes, and Dad."
"Your father knows that you have a doll?"
"Yes."
"And what does he say about that?"
"Oh, he said she was a pretty little thing."

"Blow me down!"

"It's a long story, Gran. I'll tell you when I next see you."

"Well, when you do, I've something to show you. I was tidying my writing desk the other day—it's something I've been meaning to do for ages—"

"Like the box room?"

"Ha, yes, and of course it's a very, very old desk, that belonged in fact to your great-great-grandfather, and as I was going through all the little cubbyholes in turn, dusting them, I must have pressed on a spring or a catch or something, because what d'you think I found?"

"Don't know."

"A secret drawer!"

"Wow!"

"Yes, and in it was a packet of old photographs, all of your great-grandfather Sidney as a boy, and of his sister Victoria. He looks to be about seven years old, and she about four, and I daresay you can guess who she is holding in several of the pictures?"

"Lady Daisy!"

"Yes. D'you remember I said to you, when you found the doll, that I thought it might have been Victoria's, and now it's proved."

"That's great, Gran," Ned said. "If you hadn't found those photos, I should never have known who Lady Daisy belonged to, should I?"

"Of course not. How could you?"

Lady Daisy was delighted when Ned told her.

"Next time we go to Gran's, I'll show you the photographs," he said.

"Oh, that will be splendid, Ned! To be able to see my own dear little Victoria again!"

The small pain that Ned felt was, he suddenly realized, of jealousy.

"Do you think of *me* as yours, Lady Daisy?" he said.

"Of course, dear boy. Why, to be sure, you sound almost to be jealous of someone so long dead. There is no call for that, Ned. You have quite taken Victoria's place in my affections."

"Oh, that's great!" said Ned. "And I'm very fond of you, you know. I always shall be."

"You may tire of me," said Lady Daisy, "as you grow older. That would only be natural. You may pass me on, to another child."

"I wouldn't dream of it!" said Ned.

Perhaps it was the red October sun, sinking in the west and shining in through the window of Ned's bedroom, but once again it seemed to him almost as though there was a blush on the doll's smooth cheeks.

"Dreams," she said thoughtfully after a while. "Now there is something in which we are not alike, for I do not have them. In fact, I never really know the meaning of the word."

"Dreams are thoughts you have while you're asleep. Thoughts about people or places or happenings. You imagine things in your head."

"You may. I do not," said Lady Daisy. "When my eyes close, I know nothing until they reopen. Pray tell me more of these dreams. How, for example, do you establish that you are dreaming? You may be dreaming now, at this very moment, may you not?"

"Oh, no!" said Ned, laughing. "I'm wide awake!"

"How do you know?"

"Oh, it's easy to tell. You give yourself a hard pinch, and if it hurts, you're not dreaming."

He pinched his arm.

"Like this," he said. "Ow!"

"Now pinch me," said Lady Daisy.

Feeling rather silly, Ned pushed back the sleeve of the apple-green gown and pressed the chubby pink upper arm hard with thumb and index finger.

"That does not hurt at all," said the doll. "Therefore it is I who must be dreaming. Maybe the whole of life is but a dream. What do you say to that, Master Ned?"

"Oh, Lady Daisy, you're pulling my leg!"

Expressionless as always, Lady Daisy Chain nevertheless made a noise that could only have been a giggle.

"I wouldn't dream of it!" she said.

"Mind you," said Ned, "dreams aren't always nice. Mum always says 'sweet dreams' to me last thing at night, but they're sometimes horrid. A really bad one is called a nightmare."

Which is exactly what Ned had that night.

Whether it was because he was lying flat on his back instead of on his side as usual, or because he had had Welsh rabbit for supper, or simply on account of that conversation with Lady Daisy, he dreamed that something awful was happening to her. What it was he did not know, for there was a wall between them, so he could not see her. But he could hear her voice, and it was raised in anguish.

"Help, Ned!" she was crying. "Help! Save me!" and then there was a sudden silence. He woke up, trembling.

Still half in the grip of the dream, he switched on the light, to see to his relief that Lady Daisy lay peacefully asleep in her shoe box beside the bed.

Next morning, he did not tell her of his nightmare. It promised to be a beautiful autumn day, sunny and mild and just right for the start of the half-term vacation. Ned's father had gone to his office and his mother was working upstairs, so he and Lady Daisy had the place more or less to themselves.

"I'm going out to do some goalkeeping practice," he said to her. "D'you want to come and watch?"

"By all means," she replied. "But how will you manage to do that without a playmate to kick the ball at you?"

"I'll show you."

Ned's method was primitive but effective. The side of the garage ran along one edge of the lawn, and he simply kicked his soccer ball against the wall and then saved (or was beaten by) the resulting rebound.

Lady Daisy, carefully propped upright by Ned on a garden seat at one side and out of the line of fire, stood and watched.

Conscious of his audience, Ned proceeded to show off, banging the ball against the brickwork harder and harder, and throwing himself about in a series of wildly exaggerated and theatrical saves (or gallant but unsuccessful attempts), and generally playing to the gallery like mad.

The constant thudding of the ball against the garage wall was soon matched by the ceaseless excited barking of the neighbors' dog. This was a large and friendly young Labrador, whose one ambition in life, never yet realized, was to play soccer with Ned. However, the dividing fence between the two gardens was just too high for it to leap over, though it had made many efforts to do so.

After a while the thudding ceased, for, as sometimes happened, the rebound from a fiercely struck shot not only evaded the goalkeeper, but went clear over the front wall of the garden into the road beyond. It was a quiet suburban road with little daytime traffic, but it sloped steeply, down to a point perhaps a hundred yards below Ned's house. And once the ball had

cleared the wall, it always rolled all the way to the bottom of the hill.

Ned set off to retrieve it, momentarily forgetting about his audience. Hardly was he through the gate and out of sight than, with a desperate leap, the Labrador managed to get a purchase with its front paws on the top of the fence and, scrabbling madly with its hind feet, to topple over, successful at last.

Ned had collected his soccer ball and was trudging back up the slope when suddenly he heard a voice raised in terror from behind the distant garden wall.

"Help, Ned!" cried the voice. "Help! Save me!" and then there was a sudden silence.

His heart in his mouth, Ned began to run, but before he could reach the gate, the dog came rushing out of it into the road. Held in its jaws was a small body, a body whose long black hair blew out in the breeze like a distress signal as the Labrador galloped away.

10

Mr. Merryweather-Jones

As Ned ran wildly after the fleeing dog, his mind was filled with an awful picture of Lady Daisy's likely fate. One thing was certain, that the dog could run far faster than he and would soon be out of sight. And then—and this was not certain, but horribly probable—the Labrador, which was not much more than a puppy, would treat the doll as puppies are wont to treat anything that is chewable, from a bone to an old slipper. Not much chance hardened beeswax would have in those strong jaws.

In fact, the dog made no effort to outstrip him, but lolloped ahead and after a while actually turned back and began to gambol around him. It was obviously delighted to have hit upon a game to play with the boy next door, even though it was not with the soccer ball that Ned still clutched.

"Drop it! Drop it!" Ned shouted angrily, and then, since this had no effect, he tried blandishment.

"Come along, good dog, come here, there's a good boy," he said in the friendliest of voices, but though the dog would allow him to get quite near, almost near enough to make a grab, it would then whirl away again, tail wagging happily, shaking its head from side to side as though it were a rat that it held in its mouth.

At least Lady Daisy lay flat, Ned could see. Her head and shoulders stuck out at one side of the dog's jaws, the white-gloved arms raised as though in token of surrender, and her pink-shod feet hung from the other side. But the eyes were tight shut, proof that at least she was unconscious of her ordeal.

So far the game of tag had taken place on the pavement, but now the Labrador seemed to tire of it and crossed the road in a determined manner, as if to say, "That's enough of that. Now I'm off to have a bit of fun chewing this thing to bits."

In the nick of time, Ned had a brainstorm. Suddenly realizing that he still held the soccer ball, he began to bounce it, and at the sound the dog stopped and looked back. Ned kicked the ball a little way along the pavement. The dog watched it intently as it rolled along. At last! Ned could see it thinking. What I've been waiting for all this time, a game of soccer—and it suddenly dashed back across the road, dropping the doll on the way, and attacked the ball with mouth and paws, snapping at it and barking with excitement, and eventually dribbling it away at high speed with its nose.

All the time that Ned had been trying to catch the dog, not a single car had passed, but now, as he ran to pick up Lady Daisy, a small white van swung around a nearby corner and in a matter of seconds was almost on top of the fallen doll.

Few goalkeepers can have made such a save as Ned now did. Throwing himself full length off the pavement as though it were soft grass and not hard pavement beneath him, he shot out a desperate arm, and grabbing Lady Daisy by her long hair, pulled her clear as the van swerved and braked and stopped.

Ned picked himself and Lady Daisy up. His jeans were torn and his knees and one elbow skinned, but he gave no thought to this as he laid her carefully on the pavement and knelt beside her, looking anxiously to see what damage there was.

Mercifully there seemed little, perhaps because the Labrador had the soft mouth of all good gun-dogs that retrieve game without marking it. Her face was un-spoiled, her limbs unharmed, and the worst that seemed to have happened was that her hair was mussed and the green gown dirty and wet with slobber.

Ned had got out his handkerchief and was mopping

rather ineffectually at the material, when a voice said, "You're a bit young to be trying to commit suicide."

Ned looked up to see a man standing beside him. He was a very tall man, so tall that it was difficult to see how he could have fitted himself into the little white van behind him. On its side, Ned could see, was written:

EMJAY ANTIQUES

Ned got up, holding Lady Daisy.

"I'm sorry," he said. "You see, a dog stole her and ran off with her and then it dropped her and then I was afraid you were going to run over her."

"I might well have done," said the man. "My eyesight's not exactly 20/20."

Ned could see that he wore thick spectacles, that he had a large beaky nose and a crop of white hair, and that as well as being very tall, he was very thin. He looked like a long-legged wading bird, a heron perhaps.

"But," he went on, "I'm very glad that I didn't, now that I see what it is you have there. May I have a closer look at it?"

Rather reluctantly, Ned handed Lady Daisy over, and the tall man held her up to inspect her. Her blue eyes opened and she stared into the thick spectacles.

"A remarkable specimen," said the man after a

while. "And the clothes—exquisite. No harm done, it seems—she just needs a wash and brush-up. By the way, let me introduce myself. My name is Merryweather-Jones, and I am an antique dealer. Now, I don't know if you're aware of it, but this is almost certainly an extremely valuable doll. You say a dog stole her? From your sister perhaps?"

"No, she's mine."

"Really?" said Mr. Merryweather-Jones.

"Can I have her back, please?" said Ned.

"Of course. Well, it's none of my business why a boy like you—a very athletic boy, judging by your performance just now—should want to carry a doll about, but I tell you here and now . . . what's your name, by the way?"

"Ned."

"I tell you here and now, Ned, that if ever you should consider selling that doll, I should be most happy to make you an offer."

Ned shook his head.

"I am not talking of a paltry sum of money, you know," said the dealer, and he took from his pocket a wad of ten-pound notes and riffled them.

"She's not for sale," Ned said.

Mr. Merryweather-Jones nodded.

"I see," he said. "Anyway, should you change your mind, here's my card," and he handed Ned a little square of cardboard that read:

and beneath was an address and telephone number.

"I hope you haven't hurt yourself," he said.

"I'm all right," said Ned.

"Where do you live?"

"Not far."

"Can I offer you a lift?"

"No, thanks," said Ned.

He knew that you did not accept lifts from strange men, and this one looked strange all right.

"It's only a few minutes' walk," he said.

"Very well," said Mr. Merryweather-Jones.

He turned away and walked to his van with long heron's strides, and folded himself inside.

Ned waited for the antique dealer to drive on, but he did not. Instead, he produced a large curved pipe and filled it with tobacco and lit it.

Ned turned for home.

He looked back just before the next corner, but the white van was still standing there, big puffs of smoke rising from the driver's window.

The moment Ned was out of sight, he stopped, and holding Lady Daisy up before him, said urgently, "Are you all right? Are you hurt? Did the dog hurt you?"

"A dog, was it?" said Lady Daisy. "I could not see, it all happened so swiftly. One minute I was standing on the garden chair, and the next some fearful creature grabbed me. I could not properly see what it was, just that it was terrifying, as in one of those nightmares you were telling me about. Then everything went blank and I knew no more until just now, when I found myself being held and stared at by a total stranger."

By the time Ned had told Lady Daisy everything that had happened, they had reached home. He carried her upstairs.

"Perhaps you'd like a little rest?" he said.

"I think I would," said Lady Daisy. "I feel a trifle shaken, I do declare."

As he laid her in the shoe box, he heard his name being called, and opened the window to see the lady from next door standing below, holding a punctured and much-chewed soccer ball.

"Oh, there you are, Ned," she called. "Is this yours?"

"Yes," said Ned, none too happily.

"I'm so sorry," she said. "It was Sandy, the bad dog. He got out somehow and got hold of it. I found him waiting outside our gate with it in his mouth. Don't worry, we'll buy you a new one. I *am* sorry."

"That's all right," Ned said.

As the neighbor went out the gate, the white van came along the road and stopped beside her. Ned could see her bend down to the window, and listen, and nod her head, and point toward his house.

Then the van drove away.

11

Quite a Sum
of Money

"Oh, dear, she certainly is a mess!" said
Ned's mother when she saw what a state
Lady Daisy was in. "Whatever's happened to her?"

Ned simply said that the doll had been taken by the
dog next door, and then nearly run over. He said nothing about Mr. Merryweather-Jones, he didn't know
why.

"I tried to wipe the dirt off her clothes," he said,
"but it made it worse. What can I do, Mum?"

"I think you'd better leave this to me, Ned," said his
mother.

She turned Lady Daisy over and saw that the apple-
green gown was fastened down the back with a long
row of tiny hooks and eyes.

"Lucky they made things with such care and attention to detail in those days," she said. "I can take this dress off, and then I can wash and iron it."

"Take off her dress?" said Ned, and there was a note of horror in his voice that made his mother smile.

"Of course. She's only a doll, you know that."

She's not "only a doll," thought Ned, but you don't know that. Why, whatever will she think, being made to stand there without a stitch on? She'll be dreadfully embarrassed. Ah, but wait—she needn't know, need she?

"Mum," he said, "when you've taken Lady Daisy's dress off, can you put her back in her box?"

"Why? Think she'll catch cold?"

"She might."

"Oh, honestly, Ned!"

His mother undid the top hook and eye.

"Wait a moment," she said, "and then you can wrap your precious Lady Daisy in a towel and put her to bed with a hot-water bottle, if you want."

"No, no," said Ned hastily, "I'm going across to the park. I've fixed to meet some of my friends from school for a game."

In fact, he had fixed no such thing, but when he got there he found that there were, as usual, a dozen boys kicking a ball about, with piles of folded coats for goalposts. Among them, Ned saw with some alarm, was

Troy Bullock, but it was too late to draw back, for someone caught sight of him and shouted, "Here's old Ned! Come on, Ned, get in goal, our goalie's hopeless."

Troy, whose nose, Ned noticed, still looked a bit the worse for wear, was on the opposing side, and Ned was soon kept busy saving a number of fierce shots seemingly designed to take his head off. Once the two boys collided, and as they picked themselves up, Troy said softly, "I'll get even with you, dolly boy," and ran off again before Ned could think of a reply.

Walking home after the game had ended, he wished he had been ready with a slick answer like "You and who else, crybaby?" and then was rather glad he hadn't. After all, next time it might be his nose that suffered. But he soon forgot about Troy for thinking of Lady Daisy. Would his mother have been able to clean her up?

The answer was plain as soon as he came into the kitchen. There, standing on the counter beside the Aga cooker, staring straight at him, was Lady Daisy. Her gown was spotless, and not a hair of her head was out of place.

"Oh, thanks, Mum!" Ned cried. "She looks great! How did you manage it?"

"With a great deal of caution," his mother said. "That dress is awfully old, you know. I had to wash it very carefully, just squeezing it out gently in lukewarm soapy water, and then putting it on the rack above the Aga till it was dry enough to press with a cool iron. By the way, you needn't have worried about her catching cold. Under that gown she was wearing two petticoats, one of them full-length, and under those a camisole and a pair of drawers. The Victorians didn't do things by halves, you know. When they dressed a doll, they dressed her properly. So you needn't have been embarrassed about seeing her in the altogether."

"Embarrassed? Me?" said Ned. "Oh, honestly, Mum!" and then, changing the subject quickly, "How did you manage with her hair?"

"It took some doing. She looked as though she'd been through a hedge backward. I didn't dare wash it, I just dampened it a little to make it easier to comb out; and, as you see, I've gathered it into a ponytail and tied it with a ribbon. D'you think it looks nice like that?"

"Very nice," Ned said.

"I always thought they used horsehair for dolls, but hers is surprisingly soft and fine. Anyway, she's all right now. What about you? You've torn your jeans, I see."

"Yes, sorry. And I scraped my knees and my elbow a bit, but it's nothing."

"Must be if you've been off playing soccer again," said his mother. "Here, I'd better mend those jeans. Take 'em off. I'll go and get my sewing box," and she went out of the room.

"Do I understand," said Lady Daisy, "that you are about to behave in a most ungentlemanly manner?"

"How d'you mean?" said Ned.

"That you are about to remove your nether garments in public? Because if that is the case, I should be obliged if you would assist me to adopt a supine position. There are some sights unfit for a lady's eyes."

One sight that was decidedly fit for this lady's eyes, it turned out, was her reflection in the looking glass. When he was once more decently dressed, Ned took Lady Daisy upstairs to show her how she looked in the now spotlessly clean and beautifully ironed gown. Since she could not turn her head, he used a hand mirror as well, holding it so as to reflect her profile onto the looking glass and thus show the new hairdo. His mother had tied the ponytail with a bow of gold ribbon from a chocolate box, and Lady Daisy obviously liked what she saw.

"It makes me look more youthful, do you not think, Ned?" she said. "And how beautifully your mother has cleaned my gown. I had thought the colors to be faded, but it must have been the dust of ages, for they have come up like new!" And she spent quite a time admiring herself from various angles.

A couple of days later, Ned went to a friend's house to play video games. He did not, of course, take Lady Daisy, but left her in his room propped between her elephants, in front of the television set, watching the

TV. She preferred the commercial channels, for the advertisements fascinated her.

When Ned returned home, the first thing he noticed as he walked up the garden path was a strange smell. The morning was the sort of crisp November one when scents like woodsmoke hang in the clear air, but this smell was of a different sort of smoke—tobacco. And when he reached his room, the television was switched off, and though the elephants still stood patiently before the set, they were supporting nothing.

Ned shot downstairs.

"Mum!" he shouted. "Where's Lady Daisy? I left her in my room. She's gone!"

"Calm down," said his mother. "She's all right. By the way, you didn't just leave her, you left the television on—I switched it off when I went to fetch her."

"Why?"

"Well, what use is TV to a doll?"

"No, I mean, why did you fetch her?"

"To show her to someone. Someone who called on purpose to see her. You didn't tell me about Mr. Merryweather-Jones, did you?"

"He's been here?"

"Yes, he's only just left. And he was most enthusiastic about your Lady Daisy Chain. When he had seen her before she was dirty and untidy, but now she's looking her best. And, of course, he was most impressed by all her clothes. And as for her hair, it actually is human hair, Ned."

"How d'you know?"

"Mr. Merryweather-Jones told me. It seems there was quite a trade in human hair at the turn of the century, from Italy mostly, where the girls of poor families would have their long tresses cut off for sale to other countries. Most of it went for ladies' hairpieces, but some was used in the making of the finest dolls, which were all made in Germany or France. Lady Daisy, you'll be interested to hear, is French."

"With Italian hair."

"And Mr. Merryweather-Jones is very keen to acquire her. He made me an offer."

"You didn't accept, Mum?" said Ned in horror.

"I couldn't accept it, Ned. The doll is yours to sell, not mine."

"But I won't sell her, ever."

"Well, that's up to you. But you might want to consult Gran about this, and find out what she thinks. You see, there's quite a sum of money involved, for a boy of your age. Mr. Merryweather-Jones is offering five hundred pounds. Cash."

"Will You Be
All Right?"

"Five hundred pounds!" said Gran, when Ned rang her. "That's a lot of money, Ned. What are you going to do?"

"How would you feel if I sold her?" Ned said, winking at his mother.

There was a short silence at the other end of the line, and then his grandmother said, "I'd be disappointed, pet, I must admit. We did rather agree that you would look after Lady Daisy."

"Don't worry, Gran, I was only teasing," Ned said. "Of course I won't sell her. I wouldn't sell her for five thousand pounds."

❖　❖　❖

"Five hundred pounds!" said his father, when he came home. "I can tell you one thing, Ned. If a dealer offers you that, the doll's worth twice as much, at least. You must play hard to get, keep him dangling, he'll come up with more. Just think, you might get enough to buy yourself new soccer cleats and a fancy track suit, and that terrific skateboard you had your eye on, oh, and your own video recorder, and a brand-new bike—all the things you're always saying you want."

The fact that he did want all those things did not tempt Ned for more than a couple of seconds.

"I'm not selling Lady Daisy, Dad," he said firmly. "I couldn't. She's one of the family."

His father looked at him. He looked at his wife. Then he looked at his son again.

"Okay," he said, "if that's the way you see it, that's fine. Selling a member of the family is wrong, eh? Mind you, it's an established fact that a couple of hundred years ago men used to sell their wives if they got fed up with them. A chap used to put a rope around his wife's neck and lead her off to market and auction her off to the highest bidder. Though I wouldn't do that to your mother."

"Thanks a bunch," his wife said.

"And I could probably get a few quid for you, Ned, in ten years' time, if some First Division side is short of a goalie."

"I'd be over eighteen," Ned said. "You wouldn't get a penny of the fee, Dad."

95

His father laughed.

"Anyway," he said, "you're probably wise to hang on to her. Her value can only increase, provided you take good care of her."

Ned had no intention of telling Lady Daisy Chain about Mr. Merryweather-Jones's offer. He could just imagine her saying, as Queen Victoria had done, "We are not amused." But then it occurred to him that she might have heard the dealer's conversation with his mother, but apparently she had not. She might well have used the old Queen's words, though, for she made it plain that she strongly objected to being manhandled by "that tall thin fellow, peering at one through those great spectacles, and even, would you believe it, raising the hem of one's gown to examine one's petticoats! Hardly the act of an English gentleman!"

I wonder if she knows she's French, thought Ned.

"A Frenchman wouldn't have done such a thing, I suppose," he said.

"Oh, do not talk to me of the French, Ned, I beg you! Any foreigner is bad enough, but the French! Our mortal enemies! Why, all through the centuries, from William of Normandy to that odious little Napoleon, we have been fighting the frog-eating rascals!"

"Not in this century, Lady Daisy. They were our allies in two World Wars."

"Such an alliance can only have been a faux pas,"

96

said Lady Daisy firmly, so Ned dropped the subject. Telling her that her hair was Italian would have made it stand on end, he thought!

They had just settled down to watch *Neighbours,* when he heard his mother calling him to the telephone.

"It's Mr. Merryweather-Jones," she said, her hand over the mouthpiece. "Your mind's quite made up, is it, Ned? Shall I just tell him that the doll's not for sale?"

Ned hesitated, not because he was wavering, but because he didn't much like talking on the phone, and he didn't, he thought, much like Mr. Merryweather-Jones. But then he thought, no, I'm looking after Lady Daisy, I must deal with him myself.

"No, I'll talk to him, Mum," he said.

His parents, listening while not appearing to listen, heard Ned's side of the conversation.

"Hello . . . Yes, my mother told me. . . . No, I don't want to sell the doll. . . . No, that wouldn't make any difference. . . . No, sorry, I shan't change my mind. . . . Good-bye."

"What did he say?" asked Ned's father.

"Offered me more money. Another hundred pounds."

"Told you so."

"You've got to admire the boy," he said to his wife when Ned had gone to bed. "Ninety-nine kids out of a hundred would have jumped at that fellow's offer—six hundred pounds for a child's old toy. But no, he real-izes he's got a sound investment there, one that can only appreciate. Quite the little businessman, our Ned."

"He is fond of Lady Daisy," said Ned's mother.

"Fond! Of a doll! Oh, honestly, dear!"

"I heard him the other day—I was sort of eaves-dropping by mistake—talking away to it, with pauses for it to answer, just like a phone conversation. Only, of course, it didn't say anything in reply."

"You amaze me. Since that doll arrived in this house, the boy's been living in a world of make-believe, it seems. He must get it from you—I was never like that."

Later that evening the next-door neighbor called to apologize for the damage done to Ned's soccer ball by the dog Sandy, and to reassure his parents that such a thing would not happen again.

"As luck would have it," he said, "a cat came into my garden that same day, and when Sandy chased it, it went over the fence into yours and he followed it. We had no idea the dog could jump that high, but don't worry, he won't do it again, I've fixed an overhang of wire all along the top of the fence. And as to the soccer ball, I believe my wife told Ned we would buy him a new one, but it's probably best if he chooses it himself

—he's the expert—and then you can let me know what I owe you. Tell him to get a really good one."

When he was told this at breakfast the next morning, Ned, of course, wanted to go straight down to the nearest sports shop. To be without a soccer ball made him feel less than whole, and he knew just the make and size he wanted.

"How soon can we go, Mum?" he said.

"Later, after I've done my housework, you'll have to be patient."

After breakfast Ned could not settle, but paced around like an expectant father in a maternity hospital. He could not decide whether he should buy a ball with red sections, or blue, or green.

"Do get out of my way," his mother said, as he tripped over the cord of the vacuum cleaner. "Have you made your bed? No? Well, go and do it. And wash —your face is filthy."

While he was engaged in what passed for bed-making, Ned tried to explain his frustration to Lady Daisy.

"I need a new soccer ball in a hurry," he said. "I'm out of practice, I haven't trained for two whole days, I shall lose my form."

"You will have to be patient," Lady Daisy said. "Remember the nursery rhyme, Ned . . .

> "Patience is a virtue,
> Virtue is a grace.

99

Grace is a little girl
Who would not wash her face."

"Have you washed your face?" his mother called.

"No."

"Well, do it. I'll be ready to go in ten minutes."

What with face-washing and bed-making, and decision-making, too, Ned for once forgot all about Lady Daisy, and he was halfway down the stairs when he heard a voice coming from his room.

"Good-bye then," said the voice, a trifle plaintively.

"Oh, sorry, Lady Daisy," said Ned, rushing back up. "D'you want to watch telly? I'll put it on for you."

"No, thank you, Ned."

"Shall I put you in your box then, for a nap? We shouldn't be all that long."

"No, I should prefer to go downstairs, dear boy, if you will be good enough. Would you kindly put me on the sill of the front window in the sitting room? I like to look out and watch things—the birds in the garden, you know, and people passing along the road."

"Of course," said Ned.

"You're not bringing Lady Daisy, are you?" his mother said, when he arrived downstairs carrying her.

"No," said Ned. "She wants to look out of the front window."

"You do, do you?" said his mother, addressing the doll directly. "I suppose you told him that, did you?"

"Naturally," said Lady Daisy. "How else could he

know?" but of course her question brought no answer. Instead Ned's mother said, "Come on, Ned, I'm going to get the car out. Lock the front door as you come out, I've done the back one," and left the room.

"I ought to have brought your elephants down," said Ned. "How am I going to prop you up?"

"Lean me against that potted plant," said Lady Daisy. "It is just the right height."

The potted plant was a bonsai, a dwarf tree, in this case a fig, and Ned placed Lady Daisy carefully against it so that its little spreading branches supported her back.

"Capital!" she said. "Now I have a fine view. Off you go and purchase your precious soccer ball."

"Will you be all right?"

"Of course."

"Bye-bye then," said Ned.

He did not notice that, when his mother had earlier shaken out a duster, she had left undone the catch of the window sash.

"*Au revoir,*" said Lady Daisy Chain.

As well as buying the new soccer ball (Ned chose a red one in the end, after a lot of wavering), his mother had other shopping to do, and it was a good hour before they were finished.

As they neared home, a van disappeared around the corner at the bottom of the hill beyond. It was a white one, Ned noticed, as many vans are, but he didn't pay much attention to it. He was just longing to try out the new ball against the garage wall. He ran around the front of the house to show it to Lady Daisy, only to find that the window of the sitting room was half open.

The dwarf fig-tree still stood upon the sill, but it stood alone.

13

Emjay Antiques

Had anything else been taken, the police asked when they arrived.

"Nothing," Ned's mother said. "There's nothing else missing."

"Anything damaged?"

"No. It's all my fault, I must have left the window unlatched."

"This doll that has been stolen—could you give us a description?"

Ned's mother did so.

"The doll is your daughter's, perhaps?"

"It's mine," Ned said.

"Oh. Fancy. Fond of your dolly, are you, sonny?"

"It's a very valuable doll," said Ned's mother. "I would not have troubled you if it had been a cheap toy.

It was given to my son by his grandmother, and he has already been offered a large sum for it by a would-be purchaser."

"And who was that?"

"A Mr. Merryweather-Jones, an antique dealer."

Ned tugged at his mother's sleeve.

"Just a minute, Ned," she said, and to the police, "He left his card with me. Here it is."

"Emjay Antiques, eh? Thank you, madam. We'll be in touch if there are any developments."

"What did you want, Ned?" his mother said when the police had gone.

"I just remembered—when you said his name— there was a white van when we came in, at the bottom of the hill, it could have been his, we should have told them."

"There are lots of white vans around, Ned. You can't go accusing people of theft like that. And, anyway, do you really think a respectable antique dealer is going to go around stealing things in broad daylight?"

Yes, thought Ned, *I do. It's obviously him. He couldn't buy her, so he pinched her. Oh, Lady Daisy, what a life you've led since you've been with me. And whatever can I say to Gran?*

"Whatever can I say to Gran?" he said to his mother.

"I shouldn't tell her yet. There may be some simple explanation."

There is, thought Ned. Mr. Loftus Merryweather-Jones has nicked Lady Daisy Chain.

Meanwhile Mr. Loftus Merryweather-Jones was confirming to the police that, yes, he knew of the doll, that it was a rare Victorian specimen, and that he had indeed offered the boy who owned it six hundred pounds if he would sell.

Perched among a nest of tables in his shop and looking more heronlike than ever, he lit his pipe and puffed away furiously.

"This is an absolute tragedy," he said. "To say that that doll is priceless is an exaggeration, but it is certainly almost unique, and in such wonderful condition. And now we have the worst of all worlds. I have failed in my efforts to acquire the doll, and the boy, who must be extremely fond of it, has lost it. I cannot quite think who would be tempted to steal such a thing, except a disreputable member of my own profession who knew or suspected its value. I hope, by the way, that you do not suspect me?"

"Oh, good heavens, no, sir! But we'd be grateful if you'd keep your ear to the ground and inform us, should you hear anything."

"Of course," said the dealer. He puffed some more and then said, "If you want my opinion, I should say that it's possible that the theft was the work of some little girl who was passing and saw the doll—standing in the window in full view of the road, I think you said? —and just couldn't resist her."

"I agree with Mum," said Ned's father that evening. "Don't tell Gran yet. Let's do our best to get Lady Daisy back first. The best thing, I think, is to issue a full description and offer a reward. I'm not saying the thief will be stupid enough to claim it, but the doll may have been discarded and picked up by someone else. Or someone may see it and recognize it from the description."

So they composed a notice as follows:

LOST
Victorian doll of great sentimental value.
Approximately eighteen inches tall, dark hair worn in ponytail tied with gold ribbon,
wearing apple-green gown with motif of daisy chains, with a pink sash, and pink shoes, and white gloves.
Reward for safe return—£20.

"I'll get this photocopied at the office tomorrow," Ned's father said, "and we'll post the notices up all around the place—post office, gas station, police station, of course, your school, Ned, oh, and we'd better ask that antique dealer fellow if he'll put one up outside his shop."

"I'll do that," Ned said.

◇　◇　◇

Two days later, two days of misery at the loss of Lady Daisy, he did. By now he had absolutely convinced himself that Mr. Merryweather-Jones had stolen her. He knew where she lived, he wanted her very badly, Ned had seen a white van that morning, it must have been him.

As he got off the bus and made his way to Emjay Antiques, he felt very nervous. Not that he expected to see the doll standing on a shelf in the shop—the dealer couldn't be such a barefaced thief as that. What was worrying him was the feeling that he really ought to confront Mr. Merryweather-Jones, and say to him, "Come on now, I know you've got her. Hand her over," and the knowledge that he hadn't the courage to say it. Instead he would just ask if the reward notice could be posted up in the window.

With a great effort Ned stopped himself from turning for home, and opened the shop door.

There seemed to be no one in, and Ned's first thought was that the place was on fire, for there was a cloud of smoke in a far corner. But then he could see that in the middle of the cloud sat Mr. Merryweather-Jones, smoking away and writing something at a table.

"Excuse me," Ned said.

At the sound of his voice the antique dealer laid down his pen, took his pipe from his mouth and put it in an ashtray. He unfolded himself from behind the table, came across the room with his high-stepping wader's walk, and stood looking down at Ned through his thick spectacles.

"Can I help you, young man?" he said.

"Please," said Ned, "could you put this up in your window?"

Mr. Merryweather-Jones scanned the notice. Then he peered at Ned, as intently as a heron stares down at a fish before impaling it on its long beak. But the only movement he made was a friendly one, putting a hand on Ned's shoulder, and his voice sounded kindly as he said, "Why, it's Ned. I'm so sorry, I didn't recognize you. Yes, of course I'll put this notice up. I was most distressed to learn that your doll had been stolen. I do hope she'll be found safe and well."

She might be if they searched this shop, thought Ned, but he didn't feel so sure now. The man sounded quite nice. But then he was just putting on an act, wasn't he?

"Well, thanks," he said. "I've got to go now."

Just then another customer came in.

"Hang on a minute, can you, Ned?" said Mr. Merryweather-Jones. "I'll just see to this gentleman and then I have something I'd like to show you."

While Ned waited, his eyes were darting all over the place, taking in the conglomeration of items with which the shop was crammed from floor to ceiling—pieces of furniture, paintings, books and knickknacks of

every kind—until suddenly he saw, on a high shelf in a dark corner, a collection of dolls.

Three of them were standing upright on the shelf and he could just make out that each had fair hair, tightly curled. The fourth doll, though, was lying flat, and all that Ned could see of her was her hair, hanging over the edge of the shelf. It was dark, and it was long.

"Now," said the dealer when the customer had gone, "what I wanted to—" but Ned interrupted him.

"That doll," he said, pointing. "Up there. Is it . . . ?"

Mr. Merryweather-Jones reached up and took the fourth doll from the shelf. Long dark hair it may have had, but otherwise it was as unlike Lady Daisy Chain as it could possibly be. It was dressed in a short, rather threadbare frock of electric blue that showed off its fat legs, and its face wore an expression of great stupidity.

"Very different from yours, eh?" said the dealer. "I haven't anything to touch her. These four are all of English manufacture, not worth a great deal. No, what I was going to show you was this."

He went over to a large pile of dusty old books and picked one out.

"I thought this might interest you," he said. "It's very typical of the sort of books Victorian boys and girls were given to read a hundred years or more ago. Full of stories about well-mannered, kindly, obedient, God-fearing children, quite content with very simple pleasures. Not like today's kids at all. It will give you a flavor of those times, some while even before your doll was manufactured."

Ned took the book from Mr. Merryweather-Jones's hands. It was called *Early Days*, and on the front cover was a picture of six happy smiling children playing with spinning tops. Inside was the date of its publication, 1885.

"D'you mean I can borrow it?" Ned said.

"I mean you can have it," said Mr. Merryweather-Jones.

At home, Ned opened *Early Days* at random. There, at the top of page ninety-eight, was

LETTIE'S RIDE

Here's Lettie in her coach and pair,
With Puss, and Rose, and Jane the fair,
All going for a ride.

Here it was—great-great-aunt Victoria's favorite rhyme! He could hear the tones of Lady Daisy's voice as she had recited it, and for a moment it brought her very close.

But where was she now?

"I've Found Her!"

In fact Lady Daisy was, for the second time in her life, inside a shopping bag.

No sooner had she seen the face of the thief who had snatched her from the sitting room windowsill than she was thrust into the bag, lying down. Since then, of course, she had been oblivious of everything.

By the beginning of the second half of term, a lot of people had read the reward notice at one place or another, and those children who hadn't, now saw it on the school bulletin board.

"Twenty pounds!" they said to each other. "Wish I could find the thing!"

The captain of the soccer team came shoving his way through them.

"Twenty pounds for what?" he said.

"For finding that old doll of Ned's. He's lost it. It must be worth an awful lot to offer that much reward."

Troy read the notice, grinning.

"Oh, poor Ned," he said. "Lost his dolly, has he? Bet he cries himself to sleep every night."

"You want to watch it, Troy," said one of Ned's friends.

"Yes," said another. "Remember what he did to you."

"He caught me off guard," said Troy. "It'll be different next time."

"Oh, yeah?" they jeered.

None of them actually saw Troy Bullock coming to school early the following morning. Anyone who had would have seen that he was holding a shopping bag that looked quite bulky. There was nothing particularly odd about that, but an observer might have been surprised at Troy's actions.

His way to school lay across the playing field, which was not much more than a rough meadow with a little thicket in one corner. Once on the field Troy broke into a run, jogging around the edge with the shopping bag swinging from one hand. But when he came opposite the thicket, he suddenly disappeared into the trees. And when he emerged again, the observer would have noted that the shopping bag was now obviously empty, and would, a few minutes later, have seen Troy stuff it into a trash basket in the school playground.

That afternoon, there was a game of soccer. Troy's side was playing with their backs to the thicket, and Troy himself was in top form. As well as having the advantage of height and weight, he was a natural soccer player, with good ball control and a hefty thump in either foot. Ned, in the opposite goal, was hard pressed and indeed beaten no less than three times.

When the sides turned around at halftime, however, Troy seemed to go all to pieces. Whenever he got possession, he booted the ball wildly upfield, always in the direction of the thicket.

"What are you playing at, Troy?" said the teacher who was refereeing.

"Sorry, sir," said Troy, but the next time he got the ball, he kicked it so hard that it disappeared among the trees.

"I'll get it!" he cried, and ran for the thicket.

For a few moments he was out of everyone's sight. Then they heard an excited shout, and out came Troy again. Under one arm was the ball, and in his other hand he carried the figure of Lady Daisy Chain.

"I've found her!" yelled Troy Bullock triumphantly. "That doll! I've found her!"

"Who found her?" said his mother, when Ned arrived home carrying the doll.

"Troy Bullock."

"Isn't that the boy you thumped?"

"Yes."

"Well, we must pay him the reward, mustn't we?"

"Yes," said Ned, "I suppose so. I'd sooner it was anyone else. I can't think how she got there—in among those trees at the end of the playing field."

"Pity you can't ask her."

"Who stole you, Lady Daisy?" was the first thing Ned said as soon as they were alone together. "It couldn't have been Mr. Merryweather-Jones—he wouldn't have just discarded you like that."

"It was not," said Lady Daisy. "It was that boy."

"What boy?"

"That large unpleasant boy from your school, the one that you struck upon the nose."

"Troy Bullock! Are you sure?"

"I am quite sure, Ned. There was no mistaking him. I can see his odious face now, looking into mine. What happened was this. As I was standing, looking out the window, I saw a boy pass the gate. When he saw me, he stopped. Then he looked all around, and after that came up the path, tiptoeing in a furtive manner, and looked all around again, and then tried the window. Which was, it seems, unlatched. Whereupon the rascal seized me."

"Troy stole you!" said Ned. "And now he's coming around to claim the reward!"

"Reward?"

"Yes, we offered twenty pounds to anyone who found you, and Troy did."

"Where?"

"Among some trees by the school playing field. I see it all now. He dumped you there—once he knew there was a reward—and then pretended to discover you!"

"Why, the cunning young scoundrel!" said Lady Daisy. "I trust you will not pay him a penny?"

"Not a penny," said Ned.

"Pity it had to be that particular boy who found your doll," Ned's father said later. "I suppose I shall have to pay up and look happy. I imagine he'll be around to claim the money this evening."

"Yes," said Ned, "but don't be in too much of a hurry to hand it to him, Dad. You see, I know something you don't."

"What d'you mean?"

"Wait and see."

Troy arrived looking very pleased with himself, and watched with glee as Ned's father took four five-pound notes from his wallet.

"We're very grateful to you for finding the doll," Ned's mother said.

"It was a bit of luck," said Troy.

"It was, wasn't it?" said Ned.

"Aren't you going to say thank you?" said his mother.

"No," said Ned. "You see, Troy found the doll all right, but that wasn't difficult because he'd put it there, in among the trees."

"Put it there?" said Troy in scandalized tones. "What d'you mean? How could I have?"

"Because," said Ned, "you stole her in the first place."

"I never!"

"I've got a witness," said Ned. "A lady, who saw the whole thing. She saw you pass our gate, and then stop and look all around, and then tiptoe up the path and look around again, and when you thought no one was watching, you slid the window up—"

"I never did! You're a liar!"

"And then you took the doll. This lady told me she saw the whole thing from start to finish."

"She couldn't have done!" shouted Troy, red-faced now. "There wasn't anybody around . . . I mean, I—I wasn't anywhere near."

Ned's mother and father looked at one another. His father put the notes back in his wallet.

Ned played his trump card.

"Okay," he said. "There were fingerprints on the

window and on the sill, good clear ones, the police said. But if you weren't anywhere near, you needn't worry."

"I don't know what you're talking about," said Troy sullenly, shuffling backward out the door. "Don't you go telling people I'm a thief."

"Oh, don't be frightened," said Ned, "I shan't tell anyone. I'll just say you got your reward. And here it is." And with that, Ned slammed the door triumphantly in Troy Bullock's startled face.

"I don't remember the police taking fingerprints," said Ned's mother later.

"They didn't," said Ned, "but Troy doesn't know that."

"And what about this witness?" his father said. "This lady who saw the whole business? Did you make all that up too?"

"Oh, no. She saw it all right. She told me."

"Who told you?"

"Lady Daisy."

15

Snookered

So, of course, when Gran came to stay for Christmas, she was given a blow-by-blow account of Lady Daisy's adventures.

That evening she and Ned were shooting pool in his room. Ned had challenged her to a match, as he always did, though he knew that she would beat him, as she always did. Ned was an average player, Gran an excellent one.

"Good shot!" he said, as his grandmother sank the red and lined up the next shot.

On top of the bookcase, Lady Daisy stood between her elephants and watched.

"I still don't understand," said Gran, sinking the yellow, "how you were so sure that the thief was this boy Troy."

"Same as I said to Mum and Dad, Lady Daisy told me."

"But that was just a joke, surely?" said Gran, sinking the green ball. She looked at the little scoreboard on the wall.

"You need good luck to win now," she said.

"Yes," Ned said. "Look, Gran, you can keep a secret, can't you?"

"Of course."

"Well, you see, Lady Daisy *did* tell me. It wasn't a joke. She speaks to me, you see."

His grandmother, who was aiming at that moment for an easy brown in the top pocket, missed it and the cue ball went into the pocket instead.

"Foul stroke," said Ned.

He spotted the cue ball and sank the brown.

"It's no good me telling that to Mum or Dad," he said. "They'd never believe me. But I thought you might."

He went for a difficult shot on the next ball, the blue, and missed, but by sheer luck the blue finished behind both purple and black.

"You've snookered me, pet," said Gran. "I've always taken you to be a truthful boy, and yet here you are expecting me to believe that that doll talks to you."

She played a delicate little shot with a lot of English, and the cue ball spun back neatly and clipped the blue.

"Aren't you just daydreaming?" she said.

120

"I suppose I might be dreaming it all," said Ned. "Lady Daisy says that the whole of life may be just a dream."

He played the blue again and missed, leaving it right over the middle pocket. Purple and black were neatly positioned, and now there was nothing to stop Gran from clearing the table. Which she did, neatly sinking all three balls, and then laid down her cue.

She walked over to the bookcase and stood facing the doll, and said clearly and distinctly, "Now then, Lady Daisy Chain, perhaps you would be kind enough to speak to *me*?"

"By all means," said Lady Daisy, "but I fear that there is nothing that I can do to convince you of the truth of Ned's words. The reason is simple. He is a child. You are a grown-up. I cannot communicate with grown-ups."

Gran smiled at Ned.

"I'm afraid she didn't speak," she said.

"But she did, Gran, she did!" cried Ned, and he told her, word for word, what Lady Daisy had just said.

Age is no guarantee of wisdom, but Ned's grandmother was both old and wise. She nodded, first at Ned, and then, to show she had understood, at the doll.

"Thank you, Lady Daisy," she said, "for explaining things to me. And if you will allow me, may I say that I think the new way your hair is done is quite charming."

Ned, watching, thought yet again that the color of those waxen cheeks heightened a little.

"It's just sad to think," went on Gran, "that one day you will no longer be able to speak to my grandson."

"What d'you mean?" said Ned. "Why not? Why won't she?"

"Because," said Gran, "you will be grown-up. You heard what she just said, even if I didn't. One day in the not too distant future you will speak to her and you won't be able to hear her reply. She will still be talking, but only a child will be able to hear her. As you can now, and as, perhaps, your great-great-aunt Victoria could. Which reminds me, I've brought those old photographs to show you—the ones I found in the secret drawer, remember? I'll get them out of my bag."

Ned was fascinated to see at last Victoria and her brother, Sidney. The photos were brownish and curling at the edges, but they showed the children clearly— Victoria wearing a flouncy dress with a pinafore over it and little button-up boots, Sidney in a sailor suit.

There were several of them together, looking deadly serious, one of Sidney astride the dapple-gray rocking horse, and a number of Victoria holding Lady Daisy Chain.

"They're smashing, Gran!" Ned said. "I'll show them to Lady Daisy later. Those clothes—really weird! Oh, and that reminds me—Mr. Merryweather-Jones, the antique dealer, you know, gave me a present," and he fetched *Early Days*.

"Turn to page ninety-eight, Gran," he said, and when she had, he pointed to "Lettie's Ride." "Lady Daisy recited that to me, long before I got the book. Great-great-aunt Victoria must have had a copy, because Lady Daisy said that 'Lettie's Ride' was her favorite poem. Isn't that amazing!"

"It is," said Gran gravely. She turned the pages and said, "Look, here's a story called 'Ned's Imprisonment' by Mina E. Goulding, author of *Little Sally*." She read a little of it and then said, "Ned doesn't sound particularly pleasant. Listen. 'Ned had no sister and didn't want one. Girls, he thought, were poor, timid things, just good for teasing and frightening.' Lady Daisy is lucky that you're not like that. But what a wonderful book. And how kind of Mr. Thingummy-Jones to give it to you. I must pay a visit to his shop—I love ferreting about in antique shops."

And this, Ned found on Christmas Day, was precisely what she did, for he unwrapped her present to him to find a doll's cot.

It was a drop-sided cot made of a pale polished wood, and in it were miniature pillows, sheets, blankets and a patchwork quilt.

"For Lady Daisy!" cried Ned. "Oh, thanks, Gran! Thanks a million!"

"Mr. Merryweather-Jones produced it for me," said Gran. "He told me to tell you how glad he was that Lady Daisy had been found. What a nice man he is, don't you think, Ned?"

Ned nodded. *I do now,* he thought, *I didn't once.*

"I always like a man to smoke a pipe," Gran said. "Your grandfather did. Anyway, as I was saying, he didn't have a genuine Victorian doll's bed, but this is quite an authentic reproduction, he tells me. I thought it would be more suitable for Lady Daisy than that old cardboard box."

"Oh, we can burn that now," said Ned.

"No, don't do that," said Gran. "I'll take it home with me."

"Gran!" said Ned accusingly. "Don't tell me you've started filling up the box room again?"

"Well, not filling it up, just a few; you never know when you might need a box for something or other."

"Oh, Gran!"

Lady Daisy was delighted with the new cot, which plainly was a present, not for Ned, but for herself.

"Capital, capital!" she cried when she saw it. "How very kind of your grandmother to think of me at the festive season. Pray tell her how welcome a gift it is, and thank her warmly, Ned."

She was delighted, too, when Ned showed her the photographs of Victoria and Sidney.

"How well I remember the dear children!" she said. "It seems but yesterday that I last set eyes on my little dollmother. But time flies, does it not, Ned?"

And it will keep on flying, I suppose, thought Ned. *How many more years before one day I shall speak to you and you will not answer? How awful that will be.*

For the first time, so depressed was he at this thought, he forgot to address the doll by her proper title.

"Oh, Daisy!" he said. "I don't want to be grown-up."

"Dear Ned," said Lady Daisy Chain. "You have done so much for me since first you woke me from that long sleep. You have looked after me, fought my battles, saved me indeed from certain destruction. And we still have time to talk together, for you will not be grown-up yet awhile. But one day the magic cord between us will snap, and then you must put me to bed in that charming cot and leave me there, to sleep until another child wakes me. You will not lose me, I shall still be with you, and once you are older you will find, I think, that the moment will not be too hard to bear. Nowadays, folks are considered grown-up at eighteen, I understand—in my day it was twenty-one—but in case that moment comes earlier than I expect, there is something that I insist you must do, should I be unable to ask you at the time."

"What's that?"

"Should you be selected to play in goal for England, promise you will take me to Wembley to watch."

"I promise," said Ned.

At the end of that Christmas Day, Ned's mother and father came up to say good night to him. He was sitting up in bed reading *Early Days*, while on the bedside table Lady Daisy lay tucked up in her new cot. Ned had undone the gold ribbon, and her long dark hair lay spread upon the white pillow.

"She looks very comfortable," said Ned's mother.

"She is, Mum," said Ned.

"Told you so, did she?" laughed Ned's father.

"Oh, Dad," said Ned, "she can't talk when she's asleep!"

Afterward, his grandmother came up.

"Thanks again, Gran," Ned said. "Lady Daisy's so pleased with your present. She said to thank you warmly."

"That's all right then," Gran said. "Let's hope it lasts a long time. Long enough perhaps for your daughter to enjoy it one day."

"My daughter!" laughed Ned. "That's a long way ahead. I'm not ten till next month."

"Time flies," said his grandmother.

"That's what Lady Daisy said."

"Well, just think—let's suppose you get married when you're about twenty-five, and then you and your wife have a little girl before too long, and add on enough time for the little girl to be perhaps four years old. Let's say twenty years from now altogether. That makes it the year 2010. I'll stick my neck out and prophesy that in that year somebody else in our family will be chattering away with Lady Daisy Chain."

"Oh, go on, Gran! How much will you bet?"

"Not much use me betting," said Gran. "I'll be in my box by then. But you just mark my words, pet, and remember that date. 2010."

6/17/2010

A man, a woman, and a child sat at breakfast in the kitchen of their flat. On the wall hung a calendar, open at the current month, June 2010.

As the man raised his coffee cup, his eye lit on the calendar, and he put down the cup and checked the date on his watch.

"The seventeenth," he said to his wife. "Amazing! D'you realize it's two years ago today that Gran died? And almost as long since Mother and Father moved into the old house. Time flies, doesn't it?"

His wife nodded, mopping the child's face, which was smeared with jam.

"It was good," she said, "that your grandmother lived long enough to see this messy, sticky person."

"I must have told you a dozen times," said the man,

"of the prophecy she made—just before my tenth birthday, I think it was."

"Yes, you have. And don't you think maybe the time has come to fulfill that prophecy? After all, somebody not a hundred miles away is going to be five in the autumn. And so far she's never even set eyes on you-know-who."

"Should we wait till her birthday?" said the man.

"Well," said his wife, "I just suddenly thought it would be nice if it happened today, on the anniversary of your grandmother's death, as you were so fond of her. Go on, why don't you, Ned?"

The presentation took place that evening.

All the years since the day when the magic cord between Lady Daisy Chain and Ned had snapped, she had lain in her cot, inside an old tin trunk that had belonged to Ned's grandfather. There was no need for mothballs or mouse poison, for the trunk was proof against such invaders, and only the sweet smell of a lavender-sachet wafted out as Ned opened the lid.

The small girl was dumbstruck when she first saw the doll. Then after a while she said, "Is it for me?"

"Not *it*," said Ned. "*She*. She is called Lady Daisy Chain, and, yes, you can look after her if you'd like. Take her out—see, the side of the cot drops down like this."

The small girl pulled back the bedclothes, and lifted out the doll, and held her up before her face.

Lady Daisy's baby-blue eyes opened wide.

"Who in the world are you?" she said.

"She talked to me!" the child cried. "Mummy, she talked to me!"

Her mother smiled.

"Did she, darling?" she said.

"Daddy, she talked to me!"

"What did she say?" asked Ned.

"She said, 'Who in the world are you?' "

"Well," said Ned, "you must tell her. But first, give her my love, will you?"

"Please, Lady Daisy Chain," said the small girl, "Daddy sends you his love."

"Daddy?" said the doll. "What is your daddy's name?"

"He's called Ned."

"Oh!" cried Lady Daisy Chain. "You are Ned's daughter? Oh, how lovely! To think, I am still with the family! What a happy awakening! Pray tell me, child, what is your name?"

"My name," said the small girl, "is Victoria."

ABOUT THE AUTHOR

Dick King-Smith is the author of many popular books for children, including *Martin's Mice, Harry's Mad,* and *Babe, the Gallant Pig.* Mr. King-Smith's most recent books for Delacorte Press were *The Fox Busters* and *Sophie's Snail.* He lives in a seventeenth-century cottage in England with his wife.

ABOUT THE ILLUSTRATOR

Jan Naimo Jones manages to keep busy in Grand Rapids, Michigan, with her husband and six children. She has illustrated a number of children's books.